RARE

JAXSON'S JUSTICE

DAWN SULLIVAN

Published by Dawn Sullivan

Editing: CP Bialois and Jamie White

Cover Design: Dana Leah- Designs By Dana

Photographer: Shauna Kruse-Kruse Images & Photography

Model: Brennan Szumowski

Language: English

RARE: RESCUE AND RETRIEVAL

EXTRACTIONS

Angel: RARE alpha, wolf shifter, strong telepathic

Nico: Angel's right-hand man, wolf shifter, telepathic, has the ability to see glimpses of the future

Phoenix: Human turned wolf shifter, telepathic, complete badass, loves anything that goes boom

Rikki: Human, kick ass sniper, touches objects that others have touched and gets visions of the past, present, and sometimes the future

Jaxson: Wolf shifter, telepathic, RARE's technology expert

Trace: Black panther shifter, telepathic, badass sniper

Storm: Wolf shifter, strong telepath, has the ability to see into the future

Ryker: Bear shifter, telepathic

Flame: Telepathic

Bane: Wolf shifter, telepathic (other gifts unknown at this time)

Sapphire: Wolf shifter, telepathic, has the ability to see into the future (other gifts unknown at this time)

"You need to eat something. Please," the soft voice whispered. "You haven't had anything in days."

She didn't want to eat. She was so tired of the existence she led. Tired of the agony she lived in constantly. Of the fear that plagued her when she thought of what could happen next, because she never knew what would be waiting for her on each new day. She was just so damn tired.

"Think about your family. You love them. You need to survive, for them."

Her family. The parents who had sold her so long ago to the Colombian drug lord, Philip Perez, who had tortured her, putting her through hell, and then sold her to the devil himself. She hated her father and mother with a passion above all else. What kind of people sold their child, knowing they were giving her a death sentence? Because that's what it was. She wasn't going to make it out of her prison alive.

"You've told me of your brother. He's a great warrior.

One who fights for your king! You know he will come for you. And your sister. Your twin. You have a bond like no other. They will come, Raven. You need to trust in that."

She wanted to believe her brother and sister would come for her, she really did, but she'd waited so long already. Where were they? Why had they left her there to die?

"Eat, Raven," the voice coaxed gently, as a spoon was once again lifted to her lips. "You need to stay strong. You need to keep fighting. One of these days, you will be free again!"

Strong? It had been so long since she'd felt strong. So long since she'd soared above the clouds, wonder and joy flowing through her as she spread her wings wide. She'd always lived in the moment, happy and carefree, but she'd also been trained by her brother in the arts of a true dragon warrior. She was a shifter, a powerful dragon, deadly in her own right. How had she allowed herself to be captured? To become the victim of a sadistic bastard, who made her feel weaker than she'd ever felt in her life?

She was so lost. So afraid. Utterly exhausted. She wanted to close her eyes and slip into sweet oblivion. Needed to find peace in the savage world she now lived in.

"No! I won't let you!" that soft voice cried in despair. "I won't lose another person I care about to my father. I can't! Please, Raven. Please, you have to fight!"

She slowly raised her head and looked at the young woman who knelt before her. So sweet, kind, gentle. The complete opposite of her father, the bastard who held Raven prisoner. Amber tried to save the lives the General was determined to destroy. She snuck them food and water when the General starved them, tended their wounds when she could without any of the guards or scientists finding out, brought them comfort when they had none. There were even rumors that she had managed to save some of them, liberating them from the bastard who held them. *She* was the true fighter.

"I'm tired," Raven rasped through dry, cracked lips, allowing the tears to slip free for the first time in months. She never cried anymore. Refused to give the General the satisfaction of seeing her misery. But he wasn't here to watch her now. Amber always managed to do something to the video feeds when she came to visit, making it look as if she and the others were huddled in their cells, alone. She trusted Amber. The irony of it. Satan's daughter was her only friend in the world. Without her, Raven would have lost her sanity a long time ago. She was the only reason Raven was still breathing. Still clinging to the Hell she called life.

Amber's eyes filled with compassion, and she set the bowl of soup down on the cold, hard floor. Sitting beside Raven, she gathered her into her arms and whispered, "I know you are. I feel your pain, your suffering. I know you want to give up, Raven, and to be honest, I don't blame you. I can't imagine living the life you are being forced to live right now. All I can do, is be here for you and promise you that I will get you out of here. I will set you free, if it is the last thing I do on this earth."

"He will kill you," Raven protested, laying her head on Amber's shoulder, refusing to allow her heart to fill with hope.

"We all have to die someday," Amber said quietly. "I

think giving my life for those I care about is a good way to go."

Raven sighed, knowing if Amber had the courage to die for her, then she needed to be brave enough to live for her friend. "I could eat some of the soup," she whispered softly. For Amber, she would try.

Amber held her a moment longer, running a gentle hand over the long red-gold hair that hung down Raven's back. Hair Raven used to be proud of, but was now dirty, matted, and full of knots. "I would like that."

Even though it was a struggle, she allowed Amber to help her eat, managing to get half of the bowl down before pushing it away. "I'm done."

Amber's eyes seemed to cloud over, but she didn't argue. "Get some rest now, Raven," she whispered, setting the bowl down to pull her close again. "I can stay a few minutes longer."

Raven closed her eyes, slowly drifting off to sleep to the sound of Amber's beautiful voice as she softly sang a sweet song she'd never heard before. She felt safe for now, but she knew it wouldn't last. It never did. When she woke, Amber would be gone, and there would be more pain and suffering to endure. She would get through it, though. There was no choice. As long as Amber continued to fight for her, she could do no different.

"I'm sorry, Angel. It's another dead end," Jaxson said with a sigh, raking a hand through his short, dark blond hair. "It doesn't seem to matter what I do, that son of a bitch somehow evades me."

"He's good," Nico said gruffly, rising from his chair to pace around the conference room. "Hell, he's even figured out a way to block Angel from merging with him. Sneaky bastard."

RARE was meeting in one of the large conference rooms in the office building at the White River Wolves compound, trying to figure out a way to track down Jeremiah. It had been months since he went off the grid, and no matter what they did, they couldn't locate the cagey bear. Steele was the last one to see him in D.C., but since then, he'd been like a damn ghost. Even Jinx didn't know where the General had him stationed. They were running out of options, and it was starting to piss the entire team off. His mate was lying in a hospital bed as if in a coma, even though the doctor said it was more of a resting state now, while he was entrenching himself deeper and deeper into the General's operation.

"Why the hell is he doing this?" Storm growled. "Rikki needs him here."

"He's doing it for her," Angel said quietly. "You have to remember, he doesn't know what happened to Rikki recently. He has no idea she is in the hospital. He only knows what took place before he dropped off the grid. Jeremiah is going after the man who hurt her back then, infiltrating his ranks so that he can bring him down."

"Well, he's going about it the wrong way," Flame snapped, her eyes dark with fury.

"Actually, I'm not sure that he is," Trace cut in, leaning forward and placing his forearms on the table.

"Why would you say that?" Flame asked, tossing her red mane over her shoulder as she glared at him. "His place is here with his mate." When Trace cocked an eyebrow and looked at her pointedly, she flipped him off. "Screw you, Trace. My situation with Bran is different, and you know it."

"Keep telling yourself that, sweetheart, and maybe one of these days you'll even believe it," Trace replied, as the stench of her lie filled the room.

"Fuck you!"

"Hey," he said with a shrug, "all I'm saying is Jeremiah is out there somewhere, avoiding Rikki, doing everything possible to bring the General and his organization down. In doing so, he hasn't even bothered to check in back home to see what's going on with his mate, because right now, all he can focus on is revenge. Tell me, how's that different than what you are doing to your own mate? He suffers knowing you are out there fighting an uphill battle with us, just like Rikki would if she knew what Jeremiah was doing."

"Dammit, Trace! My relationship with my mate is none of your business."

"What relationship?" he asked dryly.

"That's enough, you two," Angel li snapped, rising from her chair, placing her hands lightly on her hips as her eyes narrowed on them.

"Fine," Flame said stubbornly, through clenched teeth. "You can't have it both ways. If you think avoiding his mate is wrong, then how can you say he might be going about things the right way?"

"That's where the two of you are different," Trace told her. "Everything he is doing, he's doing out of love for Rikki. He's trying to protect her, trying to make it so that the General never gets a hold of her again."

"How is that different from what I'm doing?"

Trace sighed, leaning back in his chair as he looked at her, shaking his head. "You still don't get it, do you, Flame? Jeremiah isn't running from his mate, denying the bond. He is protecting her because he loves her. Not only that, but he also has the training to do what he's doing."

"I'm trained!"

"No, you are in training. You don't have the years of experience under your belt that Jeremiah does. Not only that, but you are doing what you are doing for all the wrong reasons."

"He killed my baby!" Flame screamed, and Jaxson watched in fascination as her eyes began to glow. Slamming her fist down on the table, she cried, "That son of a bitch killed my son! He is going to pay for that!"

"Exactly," Trace said quietly. "Everything you are doing

is out of rage and revenge. Everything Jeremiah is doing is out of love."

Flame's chest heaved, her body shaking as she glared at him. "Mine's out of love, too! Love for my baby who was taken way too soon from me."

"It's not the same thing," Jaxson said, interrupting the conversation. "Yes, you loved your child. No one here is saying you didn't. But everything you are doing is a product of the anger you feel, and the hatred. Hatred for the General after everything he's done to you."

"How is that different than any of you?" Flame demanded, her hand clenching tightly into a fist where it lay on the table.

"Because we aren't fueled by that hatred, Flame," Angel said, walking over to kneel beside the woman. "It doesn't consume us every waking minute like it does you." Covering Flame's hand with one of hers, she went on, "The team is worried about you. You're family. This is not the time or place for this discussion, but we will have it. Soon."

Flame's eyes filled with tears, and she glanced around the room. "I don't know how to exist without the hatred," she admitted softly. "If I don't feel it, I don't know if I can keep going, keep fighting."

"Trust me," Angel assured her, putting an arm around Flame's shoulders and pulling her close. "The drive to hunt down the General and take him out will still be there, no matter if you let go of the all-consuming rage and hatred you have for the man or not. We just don't like to see it eating at you every day. We don't want to see you ruin the life you could have here with the pack and Bran over it."

Jaxson's computer dinged, and he tore his gaze from the emotional scene in front of him to read the notification. "Shit."

"What is it?"

"Looks like the General is up and moving again," he growled, his eyes skimming the report sent by one of his contacts who had been keeping an eye on anything that had to do with the General for him. "He's out of his coma. Expected to make a full recovery."

"That's what we wanted, right?" Storm asked, even though he could hear the trepidation in her voice. "What Jinx wanted?"

"For now," Angel agreed, slowly rising to her feet. "Only for now. Until he can figure out who the ring leader is in the whole operation. Taking out the General will do us no good at this time. They will just bring in someone new to run his operation." Standing with her hand on Flame's shoulder, she told them, "It's late. Go home. Get some rest. We will meet again tomorrow at noon."

"Here?" Jaxson asked, shutting down his laptop and standing, raising his arms high to stretch the kinks out of his back. He'd been sitting in the same damn chair for at least six hours now, and his wolf wanted a good run.

"Yeah. With the General back in action, I don't want to go far from my family, unless we are out on a mission."

"You got it, boss lady," Phoenix said, making his way to the door. "I need to stay near Serenity, too. I'm not letting the bastard get a hold of my family."

Jaxson nodded in agreement. Serenity was valuable to the General, especially with the secret she held — the small baby growing inside of her. And Hunter, the poor little bear cub had spent his life growing up in a cage. He wasn't going back to that. No one was going to get near Phoenix's mate or children.

Leaving the building with his team, Jaxson said his goodbyes and followed Trace to one of the apartment buildings, grateful that Chase had given him his own apartment to use when he didn't want to go back to his place in Denver, over half an hour away from the compound. He was exhausted and didn't want to make the drive. His wolf was going to have to wait to stretch his legs, too. As much as he wanted to, he didn't even have the energy for a short run.

Fifteen minutes later, Jaxson was showered and in bed, slipping into sleep. At first, the dream came to him the same way it always did, seeping slowly into his mind. Whispers of pain and agony. Misery and suffering like he'd never felt before. The feeling of defeat was there. Of wanting to give up so the pain would go away. Suddenly, he heard a voice.

I don't know how much longer I can do this. I am so exhausted. It hurts so much. Why is he doing this to me? Why?

Jaxson froze, listening carefully. What the hell was going on? Not once had he heard anyone speak in the other dreams. Dreams... more like nightmares.

Please, take me from this Hell. From this crazy bastard. I don't know what I did to deserve this, but I am so sorry. I miss my sister. My brother. I'm tired of living in fear of never getting out of here. I just want to go home.

He had the impression of lying on cold, hard cement. Terror gripped him, rushing through him as he lay shivering on the floor. A tear fell from his eye, but he somehow knew he wasn't really the one who was crying. It was *her*.

Then, as quickly as she was there, she was gone. Jaxson kept his eyes closed for several minutes afterwards, trying to reconnect with her, wondering if he was going crazy. Was it just a dream, or was someone really there? Someone who needed help?

Sighing, Jaxson opened his eyes and slowly sat up, bunching the pillows up behind him so that he could rest against the headboard. He was used to the dreams. He'd been getting them for a few months now, but not like this. He had never actually heard anyone's voice in them, had never felt anything the way he felt the hard ground against his body or the tears on his cheeks. Was it real? Was she? And if so, who the hell was she?

3

"He's awake."

"How long?"

"A couple of days now."

"We are going to have to move her soon."

"It's too late."

The hushed tones reached her, and Raven fought to break through the fogginess in her mind as she struggled to open her eyes. She'd never felt so exhausted. Her body was wearing down after all she'd been through since being captured. They wanted to know what kind of shifter she was, but she had no intention of letting them find out. No matter what they did to her over the past year, she had refused to shift, even knowing taking the form of her animal could be the one thing that saved her as it made her stronger. She was a dragon, fierce and proud, and above all else, loyal to her kind. She would not give them away. If it was Fate's will, she would leave this life, but they would never find out what kind of shifter she was, or the amount of power she possessed...or would possess if they hadn't kept her so weak and drugged up most of the time.

"What do you mean, it's too late? No! I am getting her out of here!"

"Amber, you can't save them all."

"She's my friend," Amber whispered.

They were close to her now, and Raven could hear them clearly. They were talking about her. There were no other shifters down where they held her. There had been a male, a leopard, who never shifted into his human form. He'd been there for a few weeks, constantly prowling the confines of his cell. Anytime they took him out, they had to dart him or they couldn't contain him. He'd ripped the throat out of one of the scientists just a couple of weeks ago, and Raven had watched in shock as the guards shot him twice, and then beat him, nearly killing him. When they left him in the cell, just two down from hers, Raven had tried to talk to him. Tried to give him the comfort Amber always gave her, but she couldn't tell if it did any good. There was no response as he lay bleeding out on the ground. Two days later, when she came back from her latest torture session, he was gone. No, they were talking about her, and it wasn't good.

"I know."

"Please, we have to get her out of here. You said you would help me."

There was silence, and then, "I want to help you, but sometimes you have to know when to cut your losses."

"No…"

"He's right," Raven said huskily as they came closer to her, even though she was screaming inside.

"What?"

Raven struggled to her feet, and then moved slowly to the front of the small cell. Her hands came up to grip the bars tightly as she rested her forehead against them. Amber rushed over to her, covering her hands with her own. The woman's eyes were wide with denial, wet with tears. When she would have spoken, Raven shook her head.

"You are such a sweet person, Amber," she said softly. "Wanting to help all of us. I think you would save the entire world if you could. But he's right. You can't save us all."

"No, Raven! You are my friend. I'm not going to let you die! I won't!"

"Ah, shit."

Raven's gaze went to the man who appeared behind Amber, her eyes widening at the sheer power that radiated through him. Short, brown hair, brown eyes that seemed to be swirling with an emerald green. A dark and foreboding presence. He should have scared the hell out of her, but for some reason, he didn't.

"Your name is Raven?" he asked quietly, closing the distance between them as he looked closely at her.

Swallowing hard, she nodded slowly. "Yes."

Raking a hand through his hair, he growled, "Fuck."

"What's wrong?" Amber asked, her hands tightening on Raven's, as if to protect her.

Sighing, the man lowered his head, squeezing the back of his neck. "We have a problem."

"They are going to kill me soon," Raven guessed, her body sagging against the bars in defeat. "It's okay, I knew it was coming. I accept it."

Raising his head, his intense gaze on hers, he said, "I

can't let that happen, dragoness. I promised your brother I would try to find you. Now that I have, I have an obligation to do what I can to save you."

"My brother?" Raven gasped, her eyes widening as a small sliver of hope began to fill her. "You know Dax?" And then the other part of what he'd said sank in. "You know what I am." It was a statement, not a question. He obviously knew. What if he told the General?

"I met Dax a couple of weeks ago," he told her, a small grin tilting one corner of his mouth. "He's very impressive. Took out a shit ton of the General's soldiers, along with some coyotes who threatened his mate."

"Dax has a mate?" Raven whispered, her eyes filling with tears. She had missed so much.

"He does," the man said, moving closer to her. "A very sassy, pain in the ass mate, who is strong, loyal, and I am sure out there right now with him looking for you."

"For me?"

"Sable is the one who asked me to find you," he said, his grin widening. "Laying there in so much pain, covered in blood from all of the damn bullet wounds she'd gotten trying to sneak up on us at that coyote camp, but all she could think about was you." Shaking his head, he said, "She is a mate your brother can be proud of."

"Bullet wounds?" Raven growled, her claws beginning to lengthen for the first time in a year. Her fangs dropping, she demanded, "Who shot my brother's mate?"

"Raven!" Amber gasped, snatching her hands back. "You have to stop!"

"No, let her get pissed. Get fired up, little dragoness. Let that rage in. Feed off it, but make sure to contain it. You are going to need it soon."

"Soon?" Amber squeaked, her eyes widening as she stared transfixed at Raven.

"When I get word to her brother that she lives, it won't be long before he and Sable show up. And they won't be alone."

"They won't?" Raven asked, fighting the urge to fully shift. Where had the power come from? She'd been so weak for so long, but suddenly, she wanted to break the bars she held onto with her bare hands. Unfortunately, she knew she didn't really have the strength to do that, let alone to take on the General's men by herself, no matter how much she might want to.

"Your brother and sister have become a part of the White River Wolves pack," he explained, his gaze leaving hers to track warily around the area they were standing in. "The alpha, Chase Montgomery, has claimed them as his own. His mate, Angel, is head of a mercenary team, RARE, who have been fighting against the General for over a year now. They will consider you theirs now, too, because of Dax and Rubi. They will all be coming for you, Raven."

"Rubi?" Her sister. Her twin. She had missed her so much. The bond between them was something that could never be broken, and she felt so lost, so empty without Rubi near.

"Yes," the man said, chuckling softly. "I've never met her, but I hear she is a force to be reckoned with. A fierce warrior, just like your brother."

Tears slipped down her cheeks as her claws and fangs receded, and she slowly collapsed on the hard floor. "They are coming for me?" she whispered, unsure whether or not to believe him. Her family. It had been so long since she'd seen them.

"Yes," he said, kneeling down in front of her and reaching through the bars to place a hand gently on her shoulder. Raven shivered as she felt the small amount of power he pushed her way, meant to help calm and reassure her.

"Who are you?" she whispered, raising her eyes to meet his gaze. Where before it had been hard and unyielding, it was now warm and filled with compassion.

"I am Jinx," he said quietly.

"That tells me nothing."

His hand tightened briefly on her shoulder, and then he pulled away. "I am one of the General's assassins."

"Jinx, you are so much more than an assassin," Amber said softly. "He is a savior, Raven. He's helped so many who the General has wronged."

"I kill for him." Jinx growled.

"Because you have no choice."

"There is always a choice," he said, rising slowly to his feet.

"You are an honorable man, Jinx," Amber said stubbornly.

"She's right," Raven agreed. "If you weren't, you wouldn't be helping me now."

"I haven't done anything, yet."

"No, but you are going to."

"Yes." Turning to leave, he glanced back. "I will get word to Chase and Angel. The rest is up to them. Good luck, dragoness."

Raven watched him go, before whispering, "I need all the luck I can get."

4

J axson moved around restlessly in his sleep. Reaching for something. For her. Who was she? Was she real? He had a bad feeling that she was, and that she needed him, but no matter what he did, he couldn't contact her. He had to wait for her to slip into his dreams. It had been two days since she last had, and he was in hell. She was important to him. Somehow. He felt it deep inside.

It was almost morning when she came to him. She slipped inside his mind, her pain nearly suffocating him. His wolf went crazy, wanting to get to her, but there was nothing he could do.

It hurts so much. Why do they keep doing this to me? I just want to sleep. I want it to all go away.

His heart ached for her. He wanted to hold her close, to protect her from whoever was hurting her.

My brother is coming for me. I have to hold on. Just a little while longer. He is coming.

Her brother?

I can't let them see how much pain I'm in. And no matter what they do to me, I can't allow my dragon to come out. It's what they want. What he wants, but I won't give them the satisfaction. I cannot let them know we exist.

Dragon?

Oh, the Fates, it hurts so bad! My skin is on fire. No, mustn't let my fire show. Can't let my claws free.

Pain sliced into his left leg, making it feel as if someone was literally scraping the skin from his body. Jaxson grunted, breaking out in a thin layer of sweat. It fucking hurt like a bitch. That's when he realized that his woman was going through whatever they were doing to her right then. At that moment. His fangs punch through his gums, and he let out a loud howl of anger and anguish, his claws breaking free and digging into the mattress. They were hurting her, and there wasn't a fucking thing he could do about it.

Make it stop! Please, make the pain go away. Someone, help me!

I'm here, he said, trying to give her comfort, even though he knew it wouldn't be much. Hell, she probably wouldn't even be able to hear him, but he had to do something. His claws dug deeper into the mattress as he tried again, *I'm here, baby. I would take all of your pain from you if I could. Make it my own.*

There was complete silence, and then a tentative, *Who are you?*

Holy shit. She'd heard him! Either that, or he was going fucking crazy. The sharp pain that slammed into him when something was stuck deep into the base of her spine had him snarling and cursing.

Oh! Why am I still here? Why must I go through this agony? Why can't I move on into the next life?

Because you would leave me alone, sweet dragon, he whispered into her mind. *I'm a selfish bastard. Now that I know you are out there, I refuse to let you go.*

Who...who are you? she asked again, her words growing faint, as if she were being pulled away from him.

My name is Jaxson.

Jaxson. She was quiet for a moment, and then, *They are finally done with me. I can't stay awake. So tired.*

As much as he didn't want to lose their connection, he knew he didn't have a choice. She was already fading way. *Sleep, sweet dragon. I will be here when you reach for me again.*

My brother is coming for me. He said so.

Who is your brother?

A great warrior among our kind, she whispered. *He fights for our king.* There was silence, and then, *Who are you to me?*

I am yours, as you are mine, he told her. *Sleep, my sweet mate. I will find you.*

The General will kill you.

Son of a bitch! Jaxson bit back another curse as he said, *I've been chasing the General for over a year now, sweetheart. I am not afraid of him. I will find you.*

When he felt her slip away, Jaxson's eyes sprang open and he leaped from the bed, another loud howl tearing from his chest. The General had his mate, and he was absolutely certain that was who she was now. His. The General had just signed his own death warrant. That fucker was a dead man; he didn't care who wanted him alive.

Grabbing a pair of jeans, Jaxson slid into them, then

pulled a tee shirt on. Soon, he was lacing up his boots and strapping his Glock to his hip. After sliding a knife into a sheath in his right shitkicker, he grabbed his laptop, quickly shoving it into its bag, and stalked out of the bedroom to the front door. He had no idea where he was going or what he was doing, but he had to do something. His mate needed him, dammit.

Yanking open the door, he froze when he saw his team waiting outside. All of them.

"What?"

"We felt your pain," Angel said, placing a hand on his arm.

For the first time in over fifty years, tears filled Jaxson's eyes. "I have to find her, Angel. That fucker is hurting her. She's fighting, but she's so tired. She doesn't want to live anymore."

"Who?" Angel asked softly, although he was sure she already knew.

"My mate."

"Who's hurting her?"

Jaxson turned to see Rubi standing outside her apartment door just one down from his on the opposite side of the hall, alongside her brother Dax and his mate, Sable. That's when he realized the entire hallway was full, and more people were coming.

"You were so loud, you woke the building, man," Trace said, clapping him on the shoulder.

Jaxson ignored him, slowly walking down the hall to stand in front of Rubi and Dax. "The General," he said, as something his mate had said sank in. Somehow, he knew he was looking at his mate's siblings. "She's a dragon, like you. She said her brother is a warrior for your king, and he is coming for her."

Rubi gasped, her hand going to her mouth, and a low growl began to build in Dax's throat. "The General has my sister, Raven. If it is her, she's right, I am coming for her."

An answering growl started deep in his own chest, and Jaxson snarled, "I'm going to tear that motherfucker apart with my bare hands. He's going to wish he'd died when Chase got to him, because what I'm going to do will be so much worse."

Dax stared at him for a moment, then held up a fist, baring his large fangs. Jaxson bumped the fist with his own, "Let's find her."

5

J inx leaned up against the wall in the General's room, deceptively casual. He'd been called into a meeting with the bastard and his bitch of a daughter, Ebony, and was already wanting to turn and walk out. They were so much alike, he had no idea how Amber was related to them. That girl was everything they weren't: nice, sweet, genuine. She'd definitely gotten screwed in the family department.

"We have a traitor." The General's voice was low, scratchy from going for so long without using it. It was beginning to grate on Jinx's nerves.

No shit, Jinx thought, his face a blank mask as he stared at the man who had just barely managed to escape death not too long ago. Instead, it looked like he was about to order the death of someone else. Life was fucked up.

"First of all, I was told Jerome Livingston was sent to act in my place while I was…" He paused. "Otherwise occupied."

Jinx raised an eyebrow, but chose to keep quiet. Yeah, the bastard had been occupied. In a fucking coma, put there by the alpha of the White River Wolves.

"Yes, Father," Ebony replied from where she stood near his bed. "Jerome was here."

"And?"

"And now he's gone," she said, flipping her dark hair over her shoulder.

"Daughter, do you know where he is?"

"Sure. He's dead."

"How?"

"I put a bullet in him."

The General sighed, shaking his head. "Why would you do that, Ebony?"

"Because, you weren't able to do it yourself," she said with a shrug. When he just continued to stare at her, she bristled. "The guy was an ass. He was here to take over your business, *General*. He didn't just want to run it while you were out of commission at the time, he wanted you dead; and he had a plan to make that happen. So, I killed him before he could get to you."

The General nodded slowly, turning his attention to Jinx. "And what were you doing while my daughter was eliminating Livingston?"

"Getting rid of the body."

When the General glanced over at Ebony, she confirmed it. "It was a joint effort. The guy was scum."

Like she was a fucking angel, Jinx thought, his eyes never leaving the General's. He was so tired of this life. The fighting, the killing, looking over your shoulder constantly to make sure someone wasn't about to shove a knife in your back. Unfortunately, it was the life he'd been born into, and he wouldn't be leaving it anytime soon.

"Back to the traitor," the General said, shifting slightly on the bed and reaching for a glass of water on the table next to him. Taking a deep drink, he set the glass back down carefully before going on, "I have my eye on four people. Two I want watched. The other two have to go."

Jinx knew what that meant. No one ever just left the General's employment. It looked like he was about to get some sword action. "Who am I taking out?"

"The new guard at the facility in Sacramento."

"The kid?" Damn, the guy couldn't be more than nineteen. Jinx hated two kinds of killings: innocents and children. To him, this guy was both.

"He's been asking too many questions. I want him gone."

"The other one?"

"Decker Delmer." When Jinx's brow furrowed in confusion, the General grunted, "He is infatuated with one of the prisoners, and it's gotten worse. I don't trust him not to try to free her, and she's too valuable to me. He needs to be eliminated before he does something stupid."

"Done," Jinx said with a shrug. "Never liked the guy anyway."

"Ebony, I want you to watch the other two. One is in the D.C. facility and the other is in Virginia right now. You are going to have to go back and forth between the two."

"Who?" she asked coldly, resting a hand on the hilt of a knife sticking out of her cargo pants.

"I said watch, not kill."

"Damn," she pouted, crossing her arms over her chest. "Why does Jinx get to have all the fun this time?"

"Because I need you here with me."

He didn't need her there, he wanted her there. There was a reason he was getting rid of him, sending him all the way on the other side of the states. Jinx just didn't know why, and it was too dangerous to try to slip inside the bastard's head right now to find out.

"Who am I watching," Ebony asked, as if she were agreeing when she and Jinx both knew she didn't have anymore of a choice in the matter than Jinx did. The General pulled her strings, just like he did Jinx's. The only difference was, she didn't seem to care.

"Vixen out of Virginia. She's had too many unexcused late check-ins in the past six months. She's up to something, I just haven't figured out what."

"Vixen?" A slow grin covered her lips. Vixen was a female assassin of the General's. She was lethal, deadly in her own right. "This could be fun. And the other?"

The General paused, before he ground out, "Your sister."

"Which one?"

"The only one here in the D.C. office at this time," he snapped.

"Amber."

Shit.

"Just keep an eye on her. Don't let her know that you are, and don't lay a hand on her."

"Yes, sir."

Leaning his head back against the pillow, the General motioned toward the door. "You have your orders."

Jinx straightened, ignoring Ebony as he turned and

walked out of the room. Keeping his thoughts locked down tight, he moved quickly through the corridor, trying to put as much distance between them as he could. It didn't work.

"Jinx." He kept walking. "Dammit, Jinx, stop." Fuck. He paused, but didn't look back at her. "Any idea why he wants me to keep an eye on my own sister?" she drawled, sidling up close to him. He stiffened when she touched his arm, but didn't respond. "Do you think he knows what she did?"

Looking down at her, Jinx growled, "Get your paws off me."

"Awe, Jinx," she purred, leaning in, her breasts brushing against his arm as she breathed in his ear. "We could be so good together. I don't know why you fight it. Fight me."

When she moved her hand slowly down his chest, he grabbed it and slammed her up against the wall next to him, his hand going around her throat. "I told you to get your fucking paws off of me, Ebony."

Ebony threw her head back and laughed. "I do like it rough." Her eyes narrowing on him, she licked her lips. "Come on, Jinx. One night. One fuck. That's all. Then we go our separate ways."

Jinx let go of her, stepping back and shaking his head in disgust. "I don't think my dick could withstand your kind of evil."

Turning, he stalked down the hall away from her, ignoring her laughter. He had more important things to worry about right now, like how he was going to get word to Amber that her father was on to her. Or how he was going to save the innocent kid he was supposed to kill without the General finding out. And then there was the fact that he'd promised a fire-breathing dragon that he would look for his sister, and now that he'd found her, he had to figure out how to save her without getting himself killed. Taking the stairs two at a time, he grinned. This shit was normal for him. All in a day's work.

6

"So, the blue pins show all of the General's facilities you've been able to find so far, correct?" Rubi asked from where she stood in front of a huge map dotted with three different color pins.

"Right," Angel told her, pointing to the board. "The yellow are possibilities. We haven't had time to delve into them further to verify."

"And the red?"

"Those are the ones we've already been to."

"What did you do there?"

"What we do best," Phoenix said, a devious grin crossing his face. When she looked at him blankly, he told her, "We went, we saved the innocent people inside, dispensed with the rest, and blew the fuckers sky high."

"Phoenix is our explosives expert. He's pretty proud of it," Flame said dryly, shaking her head even though there was a hint of humor in her eyes.

"Hell yeah, I am!" Walking over to pull out a chair at the table and sit down next to her, he said, "One of these days, maybe I'll take ya under my wing, show you how it's done, Red. Then, you can be as cool as me. Maybe."

Jaxson heard them all, was tuned to everything that was going on in the room, but he couldn't concentrate. He paced back and forth, his hands clenched tightly into fists, his fangs peeking out over his lips, a low growl consistently in chest. His mate, the other half of his soul, was hurting. She was suffering at the hands of a mad man, and there wasn't a damn thing he could do about it because no matter how hard he tried, he couldn't find her. It didn't matter that he was one of the best fucking hackers out there, that he could do things with a computer that others couldn't, his mate's whereabouts were elusive to him. She could be at any of those blue or yellow pins on the wall, and there were several. Hell, she could be anywhere. He was sure there were more places the General had hidden. He hadn't found them all. His mate. Raven. Where the hell was she? He had to find her.

From what Dax and Rubi had told him, Raven's parents sold her to Trace's father, Philip Perez. Perez sold her to the General. That son of a bitch Perez was lucky he was already dead, that they had taken him out months ago, or Jaxson would be stringing him up by his balls right now. Raven had been with the General for the past year. Who knew what the bastard had done to her? He needed to find her, fast.

"Jaxson, you have to calm down. You are no help to your mate this way."

He heard his alpha, but he couldn't stop. He was so angry, so…scared. He couldn't lose Raven. He'd lost everything, everyone he cared about in the past. His family, his friends, his pack. He'd held himself apart from the rest of the world after that, until he joined RARE. His team was his family now, and he had a new pack with them and the White River Wolves. Raven should be there with him, a part of all of it. Instead, she was being tortured by that fucker.

The growl in his chest grew louder, and he knew his eyes had gone wolf. He wanted to go hunting. He was going to tear the man apart, piece-by-piece. Sink his claws deep, tear out every organ.

"Jaxson, look at me!" his alpha demanded, stepping in front of him and forcing him to stop his pacing.

When he growled at her in warning, Chase stepped up. "I'm going to give you that one for free, pup. The next time you growl at my mate, you answer to me."

Jaxson bared his fangs, moving away from Angel's touch. The only hands he wanted on him were Raven's, and she wasn't there. Pain like no other tore through him, and he threw back his head and howled. They didn't know, didn't understand. He'd been with her, felt what she felt. His sweet mate.

"Get back," he heard Chase order, but didn't know who he was talking to. He was beyond reasoning, stuck in that moment when they hurt his mate.

"Those bastards were hurting her," he choked out, another howl coming from him. "Tearing into her flesh. Sticking huge needles in her. She was in so much fucking pain. I've never felt anything like it. The agony. Her fear. I'm going to kill them all! Rip their skin from their bones the way they did hers and see how they like it!"

"No!" Rubi cried out on a sob. "My sister!"

A loud roar split the air, and then moments later, two strong arms wrapped around him. Jaxson fought, but was unable to move. His body shook with emotion, his mind clouded with misery. All he could think about was the pain his sweet mate was in.

"It's okay, my brother. We are going to get her back, and then, together, we will get our revenge."

"She's in constant pain," Jaxson rasped, sagging against Dax. "I can't stand it. I would take it all from her, if I could."

"We all would," Angel said quietly. "You are family to us, Jaxson. Which makes your mate ours to protect. Not only is she yours, but her sister and brother are now a part of our pack. I promise you, we will find her and free her. We will bring her home."

Jaxson felt his fangs slowly recede and he nodded, resolve filling him. "Yes, we need to bring her home."

"Maybe I can help with that."

"Jinx!" Angel gasped in surprise. "What are you doing here?"

Jinx's gaze went from Jaxson to Dax, and then settled on Sable. "I always follow through with my promises," he said simply.

"Raven," Sable breathed, taking a step toward him. "You found her?"

Jinx nodded, his eyes going back to Jaxson and Dax. Jaxson slowly pulled away from Dax and stood tall, his shoulders back, as he returned the man's gaze. "You have news of my mate?"

"She's in D.C.," Jinx told them, walking into the room and going to take a seat at the table. "Amber is the reason I found her, actually." Sighing, Jinx slid a hand through his hair before going on. "She wanted me to help her rescue another woman, but there was a catch. This woman was being held in the General's special cells. The ones he keeps hidden way below his D.C. facility, deep in the earth. A place even I didn't know existed." Glancing at Dax, he admitted, "When Sable asked me to help find your sister, I knew I remembered the name Raven from somewhere. It took me a while to figure it out. Back when Storm was taken, there was a guard watching her. Decker."

"Oh my God!" Storm said, her eyes widening. "I remember. He was fixated on a woman he wanted the General to give him. That was Raven?" When Jinx nodded, she whispered, "I had no idea."

"I didn't know anything about her," Jinx admitted. "I walked in on Decker and the General and heard her name mentioned, but my focus was on how I was going to get Storm out of there. I didn't press it when the General told me she was none of my concern. I was already becoming suspicious to him, so I let it go. I shouldn't have."

"Not your fault, man," Phoenix said gruffly. "You got a lot on your plate, trying to save the world and all."

Everything in him wanted to protest, but Jaxson knew Phoenix was right. The young pup in front of him had lived in hell all of his life. He didn't know any different, which was wrong. He was raised to kill, instead of with love, but had become a savior to man instead of the devil like his boss.

"He's right," Jaxson grunted, dropping down into a seat next to him. "You do what you can, Jinx. We all see it."

Jinx stared at him as if he wanted to argue, but averted his gaze instead. "When Amber took me to Raven, I was hesitant to help her," he admitted. "Not because I didn't want to, but because I know if she goes missing, the

General is going to know it was someone close to him that freed her. Hell, like I said, even I didn't know about these cells. Amber found them a couple of years ago, she said. When he brought Raven to them, Amber couldn't stay away. That woman has such a kind soul, but it's going to get her killed someday. The General has Ebony watching her now."

"Crap," Angel snarled, slamming her fist into the table. "I knew we should have brought her with us when we rescued Chase."

"She wouldn't have come." Jinx sighed, sitting back in his chair and rubbing a hand over his face. "The minute I heard Raven's name, I knew my plans had changed. We need to get her out of there now. She won't last much longer."

"She will," Jaxson growled, his eyes flashing wolf again. "My mate is strong."

"Yes," Jinx agreed quietly, "but you don't understand everything she's been through, wolf. She's tired. Ready to enter the next world."

"I do understand. I know what she's going through, how she feels. Things are different now, though. She won't want to leave," Jaxson insisted, his claws digging into the table. "She knows I'm coming for her. Knows Dax is. She will fight."

Jinx looked at him, his brow furrowing in concern before vowing, "I promise you, I will do everything in my power to help you get to your mate."

"But the General will know that you helped my sister," Rubi said quietly. "And he will come after you."

Jinx's gaze went to the woman, and he seemed to freeze for a moment before nodding slowly, "Probably.

Like I said before, he will know it was someone close to him, and he already suspects both myself and Amber, believing we are helping the enemy."

"What will you do?" Rubi whispered, her bottom lip trembling slightly.

"The only thing I can do," he told her, before rising to his feet. "I will help save your sister, even if it means giving my own life for her."

Rubi's eyes misted with tears and she took a step toward him. "We can't ask that of you."

"You didn't ask anything of me." Sliding Jaxson's laptop toward him, Jinx's fingers flew across the keyboard, and soon a map appeared with coordinates. "This is where you will find Raven. I have two stops to make, so I may not make it back in time to help you free her."

"Where are you going?" Angel asked, pushing her chair back.

"I have my orders." His gaze went back to Rubi. Cocking his head to the side, a small grin kicked up on the corner of his mouth. "She looks like you."

"She's my twin," was the soft response. "My best friend."

He was silent for a moment, then nodded. "I understand."

"You do?"

"Jinx is my twin," Jade said softly from where she sat next to Trace.

Rubi's eyes swung to hers, and she took a deep breath before looking back at Jinx. "You really do understand," she whispered, tears slipping down her cheeks.

"I do." He seemed to hesitate before glancing around

the room. "It will be at least two days before I get back to D.C.. My first stop is a bit more complicated than the second."

"We aren't waiting," Jaxson growled, closing the laptop and sticking it in his bag. "We leave now."

"Taking down the D.C. facility is going to be a lot harder than any of the others," Jinx said, turning toward the door. "Take your time, do your recon. I will send you all of the information I can."

"How," Jaxson demanded.

Jinx glanced back and cocked an eyebrow. "How do you think?"

"Send it to someone else," Jaxson told him. "I'm going to be taking a nap."

"My sister is in trouble, and you are going to be taking a fucking nap?" Dax snarled.

"I hope so," Jaxson told him. "It's the only way I can connect with her. She comes to me in my dreams."

Rubi's brow furrowed in confusion. "How? Raven doesn't have any psychic abilities. I would know if she did."

"I don't know," Jaxson admitted, slipping his laptop bag over his shoulder. "It's been happening for a while now, but all I could feel was pain and suffering. I never actually knew what it was. I thought it was just a dream until she started talking to me. Then, last night, she heard me when I spoke back."

"You're a dream walker." Jaxson's gaze swung to Jinx. "It's the only explanation. You aren't a strong enough telepath to connect with someone that has no psychic abilities this far away from them. Has this happened before?"

"Yeah, but not to this extent."

"It's a latent ability for you," Jinx explained. "One that is just now coming into effect, probably because your mate is in danger. Learn to use it, to hone it, and it will be a very valuable one for your team. You will be able to slip in and out of dreams, and you can learn a lot in them."

"Well, right now I'm learning my mate is suffering," Jaxson growled, "and all I care about is getting to her. Everything else can wait."

"I agree," Jinx said, with one last look in Rubi's direction before leaving the room without another word.

"Grab your go bags," Angel ordered, moving to follow her son. "Be out front in ten minutes. I want to be wheels up within the hour."

"Whose all going, boss?" Phoenix asked, pushing away from the wall he was leaning against. "Cause my happy ass is not staying behind on this one."

"Me neither," Nico growled. "We are going to get Jaxson's mate."

"I'll fucking fly myself if I have to," Dax snarled. "Rubi and I are going."

"We all go," Chase said, on his mate's heels. "We bought another plane a few days ago. My elite team goes with RARE."

"You got that right," Sable snarled, following Dax from the room. "We all go and bring Raven home!"

Jaxson swallowed hard, gazing around at his friends, ready to lay their lives on the line for his mate. Phoenix clapped a hand on his shoulder. "Let's do this, man."

Jaxson gritted his teeth and nodded, determination filling him. "Let's go get my mate."

7

Raven moaned softly, trying to block out the pain that raced through her body as she shivered uncontrollably. She was so cold. Whatever they'd done to her this last time, it was worse than any time before, and it was taking her longer to recover. She lay on the hard floor, covered in a blanket one of the scientists had given her seemingly as an afterthought when they brought her back to her cell.

"Raven! Oh, my God, Raven! What did they do to you?"

She heard the words distantly, knew her friend was near, but couldn't respond.

"Oh, Raven," Amber cried, struggling to open the cell door with a key she'd managed to steal from the scientist months ago. "I am so sorry!"

Sorry? What was she sorry for? None of this was her fault. Amber was her friend. She would never hurt her. Raven watched through barely raised eyelids as Amber shoved open the door and ran over to where she lay, dropping to her knees beside her. Tears formed in her eyes when Amber reached out and tentatively ran a hand gently over her hair.

"I'm afraid to touch you," Amber whispered, laying down beside her so they stared in each other's eyes. "I don't want to cause you more pain."

"Hurts everywhere," Raven rasped, her tongue slipping out to slide over dried, cracked lips. "Can't move."

Amber slid her hand over and carefully linked their pinky fingers together. "That okay?"

Raven nodded, crying out at the pain that sliced through the back of her head.

"Sssshhh, Raven. Let's just lay here. We don't have to talk."

"Yes," Raven breathed, so grateful for her friend at that moment. Amber might not be able to hold and comfort her like she had in the past, but she wasn't alone. That's what mattered. Just having the other woman there with her helped.

When Amber began to hum softly, Raven shut her eyes and allowed herself to drift off into a fitful sleep. Unconsciously, she found herself reaching for him. The man she'd spoken with before. The one who called her his mate. Jaxson. She wanted to hear his voice. It made her feel safe, even though she was in hell. She needed him. *Jaxson.* There was no response. Just a black void, and a soft sob left her lips as she tried again. *Jaxson, where are you? You said to reach for you. I'm trying, but I don't know what I'm doing. Please, I'm so scared.*

She didn't know why she was admitting her fear to this man. She never showed fear to the men and women who dug into her body. She hid her pain and terror from them, laying as still as possible while they followed the General's orders, doing whatever it was that they did. Maybe it was because she didn't fully believe he was real. It was all just a hazy dream, even if it felt real. Even if she wanted it to be real. He was a figment of her imagination. Someone she'd conjured up to help her get through the hell her life had become. But... she wanted him to be real. Needed him to be.

Raven felt herself drift away, slipping into unconsciousness as she called to him. *Jaxson. I need you.*

JAXSON SHIFTED RESTLESSLY in his chair on the plane, struggling to fall asleep. He had been trying futilely for the past hour and was mad as hell. He knew his emotions were getting in the way, but he didn't know how to contain them. He was so angry that his mate was suffering, and there was nothing he could do about it.

Will you let me help you?

The voice slipped into his mind, and Jaxson stiffened, a low growl building in his throat. He knew who it was, but he didn't want anyone walking around in his damn head right now. *Jinx.*

I was afraid this would happen, Jinx muttered, as if he were distracted. *If you let me, I can put you to sleep.*

Fuck, you could do it even if I didn't want you to, couldn't you?

Yes, Jinx admitted, *but since we are... pack... I thought it would be better if I asked.* The man had stumbled over the word pack, and Jaxson knew it was because he'd never been part of a pack before. Never been a part of anything.

Even though RARE and the White River Wolves had welcomed him, claiming him as one of theirs, he was having a hard time accepting the idea of not being alone anymore.

Do it, Jaxson growled. He would do anything to connect with his mate again. He needed to make sure she was okay. Alive.

Jinx didn't hesitate. One second Jaxson was aware of everything that was happening on the plane, the next he was drifting into nothingness.

You must concentrate. It may feel like you are asleep, but you are now in a state where you can walk in dreams. Reach for your mate. She is calling for you, Jinx said, before slipping out of his mind, leaving him alone.

"Jinx, wait! I don't know what to do. How do I reach for her?"

Jaxson was unaware that he spoke out loud, and that everyone on the plane with him turned in his direction, a hush falling over them.

"Dammit, Jinx. Get back here," he muttered in frustration.

It was as if he was in a black and grey void. He could see nothing, hear nothing. Trying to remain calm, he thought about what Jinx had said. Reach for his mate. Jaxson concentrated, recalling everything he could from the last time he spoke with Raven. The low, sweet timbre of her voice. Her nervousness in talking to him. Her fear. Her complete faith that her brother was coming for her. He brought forth everything he could remember, letting it swirl around him, in him.

Jaxson. I need you.

It was her! He'd found her!

It hurts so much. Whatever they did, I fear they broke me. I'm not sure I will be able to recover this time.

Jaxson wanted to yell. To scream at the Gods for what his woman was going through. He wanted to gut every single person who had ever laid a hand on her. He couldn't, not right now, but he would.

Jaxson, where are you?

I'm right here, sweet mate, he said gently, wishing he could hold her close and somehow make all of her suffering disappear.

Jaxson?

Yes, I'm here now, he said gruffly.

I've been calling for you.

I'm so sorry, Raven. I just found my way back to you. Guilt ate at him. She was in agony and he'd left her alone for so long. Tears leaked out, trailing down his face, in real life as well as wherever he was now. He didn't hear the gasp that left Flame's lips, nor was he aware when his alpha lowered herself into the seat next to him and rested her hand gently on his.

You know my name.

So, it was her. Dax and Rubi's sister. Deep down, he'd known the moment he had seen the siblings in the hallway at his apartments. Now, it was confirmed. *Yes. I'm with your brother and sister. We are coming for you.*

He heard Raven gasp, and then a quiet sob filtered over to him.

Baby, don't cry, he whispered frantically, unable to handle her tears. *We will be there soon. I promise.*

The General is too powerful.

The General is lying in a hospital bed, weak after my alpha's mate almost tore out his throat. I am not afraid of him,

Raven. Nothing will stop me from coming to you. I will kill anyone who stands in my way.

Jaxson, I'm scared. Nothing can happen to you. Or to my sister and brother.

We will be fine, he promised. *We aren't alone. My team is with us, and so is a lot of our pack.*

Your team? Pack? Her voice was weak, barely there. He had to strain to hear her, and he could feel the pain radiating from her.

I am part of a mercenary team called RARE, he told her, wanting to distract her from the misery she was in. *We are a contract team, hired to complete missions no one else can.*

That sounds dangerous, Raven breathed. *I don't think I like the thought of you in danger.*

Jaxson fought back a chuckle, even as warmth filled him from the thought of her caring. *It's my life, sweet mate. Our expertise is what is going to get you out of the General's clutches.*

There was silence, and then he heard, *Tell me more.*

When we started out with RARE, there were six of us. That has grown to eleven since our fight with the General began. I look for it to grow even more before this is over.

You have been fighting against the General?

For over a year, he told her. *Ever since we were called in to rescue Lily.* Jaxson told her the story of Nico and Jenna, and how they had saved Jenna's daughter. He told her about Phoenix and Serenity, Trace and Jade, and the rest of the team, while Raven listened intently. When he could feel her start to drift away from him, he whispered, *Rest now, my mate. We will be there soon.*

Jaxson, what about my sister and brother? How are they?

He smiled, imagining running a gentle hand over her

head and down her hair, then placing a soft kiss on her lips, wishing he was there to do it in person. *Dax is hell on wheels. I'd never seen a dragon before. The bastard is huge. And Rubi is a fighter. She's loaded down with weapons and ready for a war. We are coming for you, Raven.*

Be safe, my wolf.

She was gone before he could respond, and he woke with a howl ripping from his throat.

"Calm down, my brother," a gruff voice said. "I've got you."

Jaxson stiffened, his gaze meeting the dark emerald one across from him. "It's Raven, Dax," he rasped. "It's her. We have to get to her. I promised."

Dax took a deep breath, lowering his head for a moment before raising it to meet his eyes again. "We will. There is going to be a lot of death on this trip, my new friend. Your job is to get my sister out of there. I will light the rest of the motherfuckers up when she is safe."

"No, brother, we will," Rubi snarled.

"We all will," Phoenix vowed. "Jaxson is our brother, which makes Raven family. We aren't leaving without her, and we are going to show them all what happens when they mess with one of ours."

Jaxson let a deep growl build in his chest, satisfaction filling him when everyone on the plane did the same. They were almost there. Soon, they were going hunting, and God help any of the stupid bastards that got in their way.

8

"Well, well, what do we have here?"

Raven struggled to open her eyes. She didn't recognize the voice, but she could smell the fear pouring off Amber.

"Don't move," Amber whispered softly. As if sensing that Raven was going to try and ignore the order, she murmured, "My sister will kill you, Raven. Please, stay down."

"When our father told me to watch you, I have to admit, I was a bit pissed off at the idea," Ebony drawled. "I thought he was just being a foolish old man, because you are really nothing more than a weak, pathetic version of your mother. You have surprised me, Sister." Glancing around, she grinned. "I didn't even know this place existed. The General has been keeping secrets, it seems."

Raven sensed movement and felt Amber slide something into her hand before she rose and faced her sister. "Ebony. Have you been following me?"

Ebony laughed harshly before snidely saying, "Trust

me, I wouldn't be if our father didn't demand it. I'm glad he did, though. It's nice to see what you've been up to. I thought maybe trying to rescue Chase Montgomery was a fluke. That you didn't really have any balls, after all. Looks like I was wrong."

"You are wrong about a lot of things," Amber said quietly.

"Oh, care to enlighten me, little sister?"

"Not really," Amber murmured. "You will learn soon enough."

"Ya know, Amber, I think it's time you and I take a walk and have a little talk."

"We can talk right here."

"Not for what I have in mind," Ebony said, opening the cell door wider and stepping inside. "It's time you tell me about all of your little pets you seem to have in our different facilities."

"They aren't pets," Amber spat. "They are human beings that are treated like trash."

"They are shifter trash that deserve what they are getting," Ebony snarled.

"Just because they are different?" Amber said incredulously. "How does that even make sense, Ebony? None of us choose the life we are born into."

Raven managed to open her eyes just enough to peer out through narrow slits. She could see Amber's sister, although her vision was blurry. The longer she stared, the more the image in front of her came into focus. Long, dark hair. Dark eyes full of hatred. A sneer on her full lips.

"No, but we choose the one we lead," Ebony responded, glaring at her. "What are you thinking, Amber, defying the General the way you are? He will kill you."

"What do you care?"

"I don't," Ebony said with a shrug. "Dead or alive, you mean nothing to me."

Raven smelled the pain Ebony's comment caused her friend, but she also smelled the lie drifting over from Ebony, which didn't make sense. Why would she say something so horrible if she didn't mean it?

Amber straightened her shoulders and lifted her head, holding it high. "Do whatever you want with me, Ebony. My loyalty is not, and has never been, with you or our father. I follow the General's orders because I have no choice, but I will never stop caring about these people you keep prisoner here and all over the world. They have lives, families. They feel pain just like we do. They don't deserve what you and the General put them through. I will never stop fighting for them."

"Amber, no," Raven rasped, struggling to move. Her body felt weighted down, devoid of energy. She couldn't even lift a hand to help her friend. "Amber!"

"Awe, so they care about you, too," Ebony murmured, her eyes now on Raven. "How interesting."

When Ebony made a move toward her, Amber stepped between them. "No! She's been through enough. I won't let you hurt her anymore."

"You won't let me?" Ebony growled. "Just how do you think you are going to stop me, you little bitch?"

"However I have to."

Ebony's eyes seemed to glow, and she threw back her head and laughed. "You continue to surprise me, Sister. It would seem you have a backbone after all." Then, her gaze turned cold and hard as she ordered, "Let's go."

"Where?" Amber demanded, but Raven heard the small tremor in her voice.

"Your choice." Ebony looked down at Raven and sneered. "You move out of my way, and I will think about letting this incident slide after I spend some time with your friend, and then you and I have our little talk. You don't, we go straight to the General and let him decide what to do with you."

"Move," Raven croaked, wanting to help her friend. She could handle more pain. It was all she knew anymore. To save Amber from whatever the General would do to her, she would take a beating from Ebony.

Amber shook her head, motioning toward the cell door. "The General."

"No!"

Ebony's eyes narrowed on where Raven lay on the floor, already looking broken, then she glanced at Amber and cocked an eyebrow. "You would rather take a punishment from the General, knowing full well it could be death, than let me at a shifter for a few minutes?"

"Yes."

Raven heard the truth and resolve in Amber's voice, and evidently so did Ebony, because she grinned and waved a hand toward the door. "Let's go, then. This is going to be fun."

"You first," Amber demanded, refusing to move from her position in front of Raven.

"Amber, please, don't do this," Raven rasped.

Shaking her head, Ebony laughed. "I wonder what it is like to have such a loyal friend."

"It's too bad you will never open yourself up to

someone else long enough to find out," Amber said quietly.

"Caring about others gives them power over you, Amber. Look at what you are doing now. Getting yourself killed for someone who is going to die in here anyway. I will never allow someone to have that kind of hold over me." Ebony clenched her hands tightly into fists and turned to stomp out of the cell. "Let's go."

"No," Raven sobbed, struggling to move. Pain slammed into her and she cried out, falling back to the floor. "Amber!"

Amber knelt beside her, running a hand gently over her hair, careful not to touch the dark bruise on her temple. Leaning down, she whispered, "Everything's going to be okay, Raven. Jinx will finish the job I couldn't. You will be free someday. I know it. I feel it, in here." Covering her heart, Amber smiled through her tears. "My life on this earth may be over, but yours will just be beginning. Live it well, and always remember how much I valued our friendship. I have no regrets."

After placing a soft kiss on top of Raven's head, Amber rose and left the cell. Raven flinched when Ebony slammed it shut behind her. Then, they were gone. Raven screamed Amber's name over and over, until her throat was so raw and hoarse she could scream no more. And then, she cried huge racking sobs that caused physical pain, but she couldn't stop. Amber was all that was good in this world. She had been the only light in the darkness Raven lived in for so long. Her friend, her confidant, her sister. The only reason she was still alive. And now, she was gone. At the General's mercy, and everyone who knew the man, knew he had none.

9

"In position, Alpha."

"Ready."

"Let's do this."

"Here."

Jaxson listened as everyone checked in through the comms, waiting impatiently by a door on the south side of the facility. He'd already brought down the building's entire security system and had both the deadbolt and the lock on the door he was going through picked. He was ready to infiltrate. They were going in partially blind, something they hated to do, but all they had were the specs of the place from over fifty years ago that Jaxson managed to dig up. Who knew what changes the General had made to the place when he acquired it? They had moved in quietly, taking out the guards on the outside of the building, and now had three of their own snipers set up high in trees, covering as much ground as they could. Angel would have preferred four, but with Rikki out, Trace, Sapphire, and

Charlotte were going to have to do what they could on their own.

There were three entrances to the place, one more if you counted through a skylight on the roof, which they did. Nico, Bane, and Silver were in the process of scaling the walls right now to go through that way. "In position, boss," Nico muttered.

"Phoenix?"

"Setting up some toys now, boss lady," came the gruff reply. "Trigger and I got this. Done in ten minutes tops, and then we will take up our positions in the trees to help pick the fuckers off when they come out."

"Everyone ready?" Angel growled.

Jaxson glanced back at Dax, Sable, and Rubi before growling, "Let's do this." The four of them were going in the south door strong, their main goal to take out what came at them, and then find their way down to where Jinx had told them she was hidden, way beneath the building. Everyone else would be fanning out throughout the place, removing it of evil assholes and rescuing any innocents they found on the way.

"Go!"

On Angel's command, Jaxson opened the door, slipping inside, the others right behind him. They raced down the long corridor, not seeing anyone on the way. Turning at the end, they headed swiftly toward the stairwell only a few yards away.

"We're in, Alpha," Aiden said, "but it's quiet here."

"Too quiet," Angel agreed. "We haven't run into anyone, yet."

"Neither have we," Dax reported. "Either this is a setup, or they know we're here."

"It's not a setup," Jaxson said quietly, rushing to the stairs and taking them two at a time to the lower levels of the building. "I trust Jinx with my life."

"Do you trust him with my sister's?" Rubi asked, on his heels.

"I don't trust anyone with my mate," Jaxson growled, leaping over the railing to land a whole floor down.

"Me neither," Dax snarled, following him down. "Something isn't right."

"Found what looks like the General's hospital room," Ryker snarled. "The fucker's gone. Looks like he left in a hurry."

"They knew we were coming," Silver growled.

"No, I don't think they did," Chase said thoughtfully. "There's still ice in this cup. They must have some sort of security further away from the building that we missed. I bet they left the soldiers outside thinking they would fight us off and give them more time to run."

"Fuck!" Jaxson snarled, leaping over the side of another railing to scale the stairs faster. "How the hell did they get out of here?"

"I don't know, but this place is a fucking ghost town," Xavier put in. "Shit's not right."

"Get out," Angel ordered darkly. "Everyone, they have to have some kind of failsafe in case something like this happens. I don't trust it. Get out, now."

"I'm not going anywhere without Raven!" Jaxson snarled.

"You got that right, wolf!" Dax ground out next to him. "Everyone else, go. We will find my sister."

"Bullshit," Sable growled, following them deeper underground.

"Dammit, Jaxson, I am ordering you. Get the hell out of there, now!"

Jaxson had never defied a direct order in his life, but he was about to. There was no way he was leaving his mate to die in this place. "Sorry, Angel. Can't do it. She's here. I know she is."

"They could have taken her with them."

"They didn't," he said in complete certainty.

"How do you know?" Chase demanded.

"I can feel her."

"I feel her, too!" Rubi cried, rubbing at her chest. "Oh, the fates! She's in so much pain!"

"Angel and I will go down with them," Chase decided. "Everyone else, get the hell out of here. Cover us from the outside."

"I don't like this," Bane muttered. "I'm coming with you."

"Bane, stand down," Angel growled.

"No can do, boss. You can reprimand me later, but something is pulling me down these stairs. I couldn't go back up, even if I wanted to."

"Storm and I are coming with you, too, Angel."

"Well, fuck!" Angel snarled, and Jaxson knew she was beyond pissed. They were going to get an ass chewing if they got out of this alive. "Why don't you all come? We'll make it one big fucking party!"

Jaxson ignored them, putting on a burst of speed when he reached the very bottom of the stairs. It was dark, dank, and cold as hell down there, and rage filled him at the thought of Raven being held in a place like this. He needed to get to her.

"Over there!" Rubi cried when they entered another room that ran half the length of the building.

Jaxson looked at the wall lined with what looked like jail cells, and his heart began to pound when he saw they were all empty, except for the very last one. There was someone lying on the floor in the back of it, and they didn't look like they were moving.

"Raven!" he hollered, sprinting across the room and grasping the bars tightly, praying it was her. He tried to yank the door open, but it wouldn't budge.

"Move, wolf," Dax growled, grasping the bars and pulling on them with a large roar.

"Raven! Oh, Raven! What have they done to you?"

The woman slowly opened her eyes, and Jaxson found himself staring into amber ones, identical to Rubi's, except they were dulled with pain. She blinked them once, then again, and he watched as a tear slipped free, but still, she didn't move.

"Raven, we're here. We're going to get you out of there," Jaxson promised.

"I can't budge the fucking thing," Dax snarled. "Maybe if I shift."

"No!" Raven gasped hoarsely, reaching out toward them. She cried out, more tears coming as she whispered, "No shifting. He doesn't know what we are."

"He's gone, little sister," Dax promised. "He won't find out."

"Cameras," she rasped. "He's watching us. Always watching, except when my friend messes with them."

"I don't give a fuck if he knows what we are," Dax snarled. "I'm getting you out of there!"

"No!" she cried, holding open her hand slowly. "Key."

"Shit, how are we going to get it?" Rubi asked when Raven's eyes closed weakly.

"There's got to be something around here we can use," Bane said as he came into the room and crossed over to them. He paused, sniffing slightly, his eyes narrowing on Raven. Getting closer to them, he inhaled deeply, then asked, "Who else has been here?"

Raven opened her eyes, licking her dry lips, before whispering, "Amber and her sister."

"Sister?"

"Ebony," Angel clarified, stalking over to them. Squatting down in front of the cell, she looked at Raven. "Raven, I'm Angel, Jaxson's alpha."

"Jaxson," Raven breathed, tears filling her eyes again. "He's real?"

"I'm right here, baby."

Her gaze moved over to him, and she reached for him, crying out in pain.

"Shhh, it's going to be okay," Jaxson whispered. "We're going to get you out of there."

"You came for me."

"Always," he promised.

Raven gulped, her eyes going from him to Angel. "You all came. He said you would."

"You better believe it," Angel said, smiling gently. "We never leave family behind. Now, let's figure out how to get you on the right side of these bars, okay?" When Raven agreed, she asked, "Do you think you can move closer to us, Raven?"

Raven nodded weakly, and then began to move toward them, sliding her body along the hard floor, inch by slow painful inch. When Jaxson would have protested, Angel placed a hand on his arm. "There is no other way," she said quietly. "We need to get out of here now. She's in too much pain to throw it over, and no one here has found anything to get it with."

"But she's hurting," Jaxson protested.

"My sister is strong," Rubi whispered, moving in close to him. "She can do this."

"I hope she hurries," Nico said, entering the room with Flame and Silver. "This place is wired to blow, and I'm not talking about Phoenix's toys."

"Go!" Raven demanded, through tears of pain. "I won't have all of you giving your lives for me. I can't be the cause of any more death."

"No!" Rubi cried, grasping the bars in front of her. "Fight, sister. For me. For us. I need you!"

"Fuck that!" Jaxson snarled, baring his teeth. "I am not leaving here without you!"

She stared at him, eyes wide, and then rested her head against the floor for a moment. When her gaze met his again, it was full of determination. "You won't have to," she vowed, beginning to slide across the floor toward him again. Her eyes never left his as she moved, even though he could tell how much pain she was in, could smell it.

"I am so fucking proud of you, mate," he growled, reaching toward her through the bars. "You are amazing. A fighter. Mine."

Raven gritted her teeth and pushed forward with her feet, fighting her way to him, and suddenly she was there. "Jaxson," she gasped when their fingers touched. She dropped the key to the floor, resting her forehead on it. "I made it."

"Damn right you did, little sister," Dax said, slipping

his hand inside the cell to touch her head. "I'm proud of you, too."

Jaxson grabbed the key and stood, quickly shoving it into the lock and turning it. Moments later, he was kneeling beside his mate, afraid to touch her. There was blood everywhere, some dried, some seeping through incisions on her body. "Is this from the yesterday?"

"Yes," she whispered. "They aren't healing."

"You need to shift," Angel said, kneeling down on her other side.

"Not here," Raven protested, with a small shake of her head. "I will never give that bastard the satisfaction of letting him know what kind of shifter I am. Screw him!"

"There's my sister!" Rubi said, with a small fist bump in the air, before she knelt down next to Jaxson. "What do you say we get out of here, Raven? I'm ready to go home."

Raven nodded weakly, reaching for Jaxson. "Yes, please."

"Boss lady, you have five minutes to get the hell out of there before the place goes boom," Phoenix yelled through the comms. "I found the General's bomb, but this baby is special made. If I touch it, your five minutes could turn into zero quickly."

Jaxson slipped his hands under Raven, gently turning her over and lifting her into his arms. He swore when she screamed in pain, swearing again when her face twisted in agony. "Fuck, baby. I'm so sorry."

"Jaxson, run!" Angel yelled, following Flame and Silver out of the room and up the stairs.

Holding Raven close, Jaxson ran. It tore him up inside every time she cried out in pain, but he blocked it out and flew up the stairs three at a time, Sable and Rubi in front of him, Dax and Bane bringing up the rear. No sooner did they make it out into the open, then the bomb detonated and the building seemed to implode in on itself.

"Run!" Chase yelled, racing away from the wreckage, his pack on his heels. Jaxson soon realized why there were more explosions as loud chaos splitting the air. Phoenix's toys had come out to play, too.

"Holy shit!" Sable yelled, running alongside him. "Overkill much, Phoenix?"

"I have no idea what you are talking about," Phoenix hollered with a grin, streaking past them.

It was ten more minutes before they were far enough away from the destruction that Angel felt safe enough for them to slow their pace, and another fifteen before they came across the vehicles they'd hidden when they first arrived. Jaxson climbed into the middle of one of the SUVs, holding his mate close as he waited for everyone else to pile in. Bane slid in beside him and slammed the door shut, and soon they were on their way to the airport.

Jaxson glanced down, and found himself staring into wide, brightly shining amber eyes. A tear slipped out, and he leaned down and caught it with his lips. "What is it, baby? Are you in pain?" Shaking his head, he sighed. "Stupid question. I know you are. I can feel how much you hurt."

"It's not that," Raven whispered, a soft sob in her throat. "I think the General is going to kill my friend. She got me through everything, Jaxson. She held me when I was hurting, made me eat and drink when I didn't want to. Made me fight when I just wanted to give up. She's the kindest person I know, and she is going to die because of me. Because her sister caught her trying to help me after the last time the scientists hurt me."

"You're talking about Amber, aren't you?" Angel ask quietly from the front seat.

Raven's eyes flew to hers, and she winced in pain. "Yes. I know she's the General's daughter, but she's a good person."

"We know," Jaxson promised her, kissing her gently on the top of her head.

"You do?"

Raven's eyes came back to his, and he couldn't resist dropping a kiss on her lips. "Yes, she's helped us in the past, too. She saved Steele and Storm when they were being held prisoner in Alaska and experimented on not too long ago."

"And she helped me," Chase said from the driver's seat. "She saved me, like she saved you, Raven. We aren't going to just sit back and let the General take her life."

"It might be too late," Raven whispered, burying her head in Jaxson's chest and letting her eyes drift shut as she thought about her friend. "Amber was standing between us. Ebony wanted to hurt me, but Amber wouldn't move. Ebony gave her a choice, either move or she would take her to the General and let him decide her punishment for helping me." More tears leaked out as she told them, "Amber chose the General."

"**G**et her prepped for surgery, now!"

"Yes, doctor."

"I want..."

Raven tuned out whatever else was said. She lay still, listening to the voices around her, but not comprehending their words as terror filled her while she waited for the first slice into her skin. She felt the cold metal against her back, and a bright light shone down on her from above, blinding her. She didn't recognize the voices or scents of the people in the room, but that wasn't anything new. The General was constantly changing employees. There was a new face torturing her every other week. When she felt a hand on her arm, she began to struggle. Pain shot through her stomach, and she screamed his name long and loud, the man she knew would save her. Somehow, he would come. "Jaxson!"

"Hush, Raven," a soft voice said, that hand rubbing her arm gently. "You're safe now."

Safe? She wouldn't be safe until *he* was in the room.

Where was he? "Jaxson!" she screamed again, the sound ripping from her raw throat as she tried to pull away from the woman's soothing touch. She didn't want to be soothed by someone who was getting ready to dig into her. She wanted her mate, needed him. He was the only one who would make her feel safe. "Jaxson!"

"What the hell is going on in here?" Raven stiffened in fear, her entire body shaking at the deep voice.

"Jaxson," Raven sobbed, moving to scramble off the cold metal table. She gasped when her legs buckled underneath her, crying out in pain when she fell to the floor.

"Raven, please, you have to calm down. You're going to hurt yourself."

Hurt herself? Didn't they know she was always in pain? It never went away, no matter how long in between their visits. Then she paused in confusion. Why would they care? The scientists had never cared before. They inflicted as much pain as they wanted, never worried about how she felt or how it affected her.

"Back away from her, Jade," the deep, male voice ordered. "She's confused. She might hurt you on accident."

Raven almost laughed at that. She couldn't fight her way out of a wet paper sack, how was she going to hurt the woman?

"Tell us what you need, Raven. We'll get it for you."

Would they? There was only one way to find out. Lifting her head, she stared at the man in front of her, frowning when she saw that he looked familiar. "Jaxson," she whispered, her entire body shaking in fear. "I need Jaxson."

"Raven? Baby, I'm right here."

Her gaze went to the man who stood in the open doorway, and her breath caught in her throat. It was him. She would recognize his voice any day. As she stared at him, her memory slowly started to come back. He'd come for her with his team and his pack, just like he said he would. Dax and Rubi had been with him, too. They'd saved her.

"Jaxson?"

He slowly crossed the room and knelt in front of her, reaching out to trail a finger softly down her face. "I'm right here, sweet mate," he said, leaning over to nuzzle her cheek gently with his. "You're safe."

When he pulled back to look at her, she raised her hand to cup his hard jaw. He was beautiful, with short, dark blonde hair, hazel eyes, and a smile that made her heart flutter. And he was hers. "I am now," she whispered.

"Jaxson, we need her back on the table," the doctor said softly. When Raven glanced in her direction, the woman smiled and squatted down beside her. "Hey, Raven. I'm Doc Josie, the doctor for the White River Wolves. I promise, I'm not trying to hurt you, and I am so sorry that we scared you."

"You were going to cut into me," Raven whispered softly, swallowing hard and moving toward Jaxson. "Like the scientists do."

"Not to hurt you, sweet dragon," the doctor said gently. "To help you." Standing, she motioned for Jaxson to help Raven up as she went on, "It seems whatever they did to you this last time left some places inside you that I need to stitch up. You have internal bleeding, which is one of the reasons you aren't healing on your own."

Jaxson gathered her in his arms and stood, moving back toward the surgery table, and Raven shook her head wildly. "Please, I can't."

Doc Josie looked from the table to Raven and asked quietly, "Is it the surgery you object to, or the table we are doing it on, Raven?"

Her lips trembling, Raven whispered, "The table they strapped me to was cold, metal, and scary. The things they did to me after they strapped me down... just being on one like it terrifies me." A shudder ran through her, and she buried her face in Jaxson's chest. "Please, don't put me on that table."

The doctor was silent for a minute, and then seemed to make a decision. "Bring one of the hospital beds in here."

"But... doctor," a nurse protested, and Doc Josie glared at her.

"Are you going to tell me how to run my practice? Because if you are, then you might want to find a new place to work."

"No, ma'am," the nurse whispered, turning and leaving the room quickly.

"Not quite as sterile as I would like, but it will do," the doctor said, winking in Raven's direction. "Would you like Jaxson to stay in here with you? I'm going to put you under so you don't feel anything, but if knowing he's near will give you peace, then he can stay."

Somehow, Raven knew the doctor was going against all of her beliefs right now for her, but she couldn't stop herself from nodding. "Yes, please; if it's okay with Jaxson?"

"I'm not going anywhere," Jaxson promised gruffly, holding her close.

"I'll need you to put on some scrubs and wash up, Jaxson. We are actually going to move this into the next room over now since this one has been contaminated."

"We're shifters, Doc," Jaxson said, his lips pulling into another one of those grins she was growing to love.

"Doesn't mean we have to be dirty, now does it?" Doc Josie said primly, making a small smile of her own appear on Raven's lips.

"Thank you," Raven whispered. "I'm sorry I'm being so difficult."

"Sweet dragon, I think you have earned the right to be as difficult as you want right now. You've been through more than I could ever imagine. Let me help you. I just want to make you stop hurting."

"I don't know what that's like anymore," Raven admitted. "I've been in pain for so long."

A muscle in the doctor's jaw ticked, but she smiled. "Hopefully, you will in a few days."

Raven closed her eyes, snuggling close to Jaxson, breathing in his scent. It calmed her. She loved the way he made her feel — safe and treasured. They may have just met, but she knew deep down that he had just become her reason for living.

11

"I want a shower," Raven insisted, sliding the blankets off and slipping her legs over the side of the bed.

"Doc Josie said she doesn't want you to move for three days, Raven."

"It's been two and a half," Raven argued, "and I am starting to feel better already." It was a lie, and she knew Sable and her sister would scent it, but she didn't care. She was used to the pain. There was always aching and soreness. Right now, she was more worried about washing the filth from her body and trying to get the rats nest out of her hair. "Look, either help me, or I will do it myself."

"Where did the sweet part of you go that everyone keeps mentioning?" Sable teased, her eyes lit with laughter.

"I could have told you that wouldn't last long," Rubi said, sliding an arm around Raven's waist to help her to her feet. "She's a damn dragon, Sable. We are all stubborn as hell."

"I think it's a shifter thing in general," Doc Josie said, breezing into the room. "What exactly are you doing out of bed, Raven?"

Raven gritted her teeth and began to move gingerly toward the bathroom with Rubi's help. "I'm tired of being dirty. I want a shower."

"You'll have to be able to stand longer than five minutes for that to happen," the doctor said dryly.

"Maybe we should call Jaxson," Sable suggested, waggling her eyebrows at Raven. "I bet he would have no problem helping you get clean."

Raven's cheeks turned a deep red as her body temperature began to rise. The man could definitely get her blood moving. "I want him to look at me," she admitted softly.

"Oh, honey, he's looking," Sable promised. "That man has got it bad for you."

"But... I feel like he doesn't see me," she whispered.

"What do you mean?" Rubi asked in confusion.

"You think he sees a victim, someone he needs to take care of and protect, not a strong beautiful woman," Doc Josie said softly. "You want him to see the real you."

A tremulous smile crossed Raven's lips and she nodded. "Yes. It's been so long since I've had a hot shower. I have dirt in places there should never be dirt. My fingernails are horrible. I don't even know if I can get a brush through my hair, no matter how much conditioner I use. I'm afraid we might have to cut it, and I don't want to do that. My skin is so dry and flaky." Pausing, Raven met the doctor's gaze and said, "I just want to feel like *me* again."

Doc Josie smiled in understanding, "I'll tell you what.

I'll get a stool to put in the shower for you to sit on. Your sister can help you, but I want her with you at all times."

Excitement poured into her, and Raven nodded in agreement. "That works for me."

"Raven?" Doc Josie paused before saying, "Tell me the truth."

"Yeah, Doc?"

"On a scale of one to ten, how much pain are you in right now? One being not much and ten being the worse?"

Raven sighed, ducking her head, knowing she couldn't lie to the woman. "To me, I would say a seven."

"Because you are used to it? You don't know what it is like not to be in pain anymore?" When Raven nodded, she asked, "How do you think a normal shifter would rate the pain?"

Leaning into her sister, Raven whispered honestly, "At least a twelve."

When Rubi gasped in dismay, Raven smiled, "I'm okay, Sis, I promise. Right now, I just really want a shower. I'm not worried about the pain. I can live with it for the rest of my life if it means I get to be free."

"Maybe after you shift, it will help," Sable suggested quietly.

Raven shrugged, resting her head on Rubi's shoulder as they moved slowly to the bathroom. "I don't know. I haven't shifted in at least a year. We can try it and see."

"I think you better wait at least another week for that," Doc Josie said. "Let's try to get the pain under a five first if possible, and make sure everything on the inside is healing."

"Sounds good to me," Raven agreed. She missed her dragon, but had no desire to shift right now. She was sure the pain would be unbearable, however, she would try if that's what everyone wanted from her. But, before she did anything else, she was getting in the shower.

TWO HOURS LATER, Raven sat in her hospital bed, utterly exhausted. She'd showered, brushed her teeth, clipped her raggedy nails, and then sat for over an hour while Rubi and Sable worked on her hair, listening to them talk about things that she couldn't even begin to comprehend. The way they tugged and pulled on her hair while trying to comb through it not only hurt, but it was making her physically ill. She kept quiet, because she had no desire to cut it. She wanted to be beautiful for her mate, not hairless. Although, at the rate they were going, she wondered if she was going to have any hair left when they were through.

"I think we need to take a break," Rubi said quietly, setting her brush aside. Raven raised a hand and ran it over her hair. When she felt the knotted mess, she opened her mouth to urge them to continue, but Sable was setting her brush down, too.

"Raven, it's time you get some rest. I need to go check in with my alpha, but Dax and I will be back later to see you."

"Where is Dax?" Raven asked. Her brother had hardly left her side since she'd been brought to the Whiter River Wolves compound, and neither had Jaxson, but now they were both mysteriously missing. When Jaxson left that morning, all he'd said was that he had some things he needed to do, but that he would be back in the afternoon.

Not wanting to pry, she'd kept quiet, but when Dax left not long after, she'd begun to wonder if something else was going on.

Avoiding her gaze, Sable stood and smiled. "He said something about working, which is what I need to be doing. Get some rest, Raven. We'll be back this evening."

Even though Raven couldn't scent a lie from her, she had a feeling Sable had just somehow evaded telling her the full truth.

"I need to go, too, Raven." Leaning down, Rubi kissed her cheek. "I'm so glad you're home, Sis. I've missed you so much."

"Why are you leaving?" Raven whispered, afraid it might sound as if she was whining. She hadn't been alone since she'd been in the hospital, and even though it made no sense, the thought kind of scared her. She'd been alone so much during the past year, she had no desire to be now.

"Sweetie, you need to get some rest."

"All I've been doing is resting," Raven argued, close to tears.

Rubi's eyes narrowed and she raised an eyebrow. "You okay?"

Before Raven could respond, a young woman breezed into the room, her bright green eyes sparkling with warmth. "Of course, she's not okay, Rubi," she said, taking a seat in the chair next to the bed. "But we are going to work on that."

The minute she spoke, Raven knew who she was, and shame filled her when she remembered how she'd acted in the operating room. All of the time the General had her, she'd never once screamed and cried the way she did in that room. She'd kept quiet, stoic, never letting anyone know how much they hurt her. But she had reached her limit and let her fear show that day. "I am so sorry," Raven whispered, clutching the covers tightly.

"You have absolutely nothing to be sorry about," the woman said kindly. Her gaze going to Rubi, she smiled. "Don't worry, I will take care of your sister while you are gone."

"Jade, she's been through so much."

Jade reached over, covering one of Raven's hands with her own. "I know exactly what she's been through, Rubi, and I'm here to help. That's all. I promise."

Raven sighed when the feeling of warmth and comfort began to seep into her body, into her soul. She'd never felt anything like it. "What are you doing?"

"Helping."

Raven's eyes filled with tears, and she laid back against her pillow, turning her head to look at the woman. "Thank you. I don't know why I am so afraid to be alone."

Rubi gasped, moving back toward the bed. "I didn't know, Raven. I can stay. I would never leave you alone if you are afraid. I'll call the alpha and let him know I can't make it right now."

"No," Jade said, her eyes never leaving Raven. "You will go to your meeting with him and the others. It's important. I'll stay with Raven. We have a lot to talk about."

"Raven…"

"It's all right," Raven whispered. "I'm fine now. Go to your meeting with your alpha."

"Our alpha," Jade said.

"What?"

"As Dax and Rubi's sister, and Jaxson's mate, you are family, Raven. Pack."

"But I'm a dragon."

Jade chuckled, bringing her other hand up to cover the one of Raven's she held. "We don't discriminate in our pack. We have wolves, bears, dragons."

Raven's eyes widened in surprise. "You do?"

"There's a lot of magic in our pack," Jade murmured, gently running a hand down Raven's arm. Raven closed her eyes as she felt the woman push more of her power into her, the pain in her body seeming to subside somewhat as a peacefulness entered her.

"Magic?"

"Yes. Isn't magic a wonderful thing?"

"I don't know much about it," Raven admitted, although the idea of it had always intrigued her.

"Of course, you do, Raven," Jade said, smiling as she leaned closer. "Isn't it magical when you merge with your dragon, spread your wings, and soar above the clouds? Don't you feel it then?"

"It's been so long," Raven whispered. "I've missed it, but I had to be careful. I couldn't shift. Couldn't let him see me in that form."

"The General." It wasn't a question. Jade knew exactly who she was talking about.

"Yes. He didn't know what kind of shifter I was. There were so many needles. So many tests. He was determined to find out."

"But you didn't give him the satisfaction, did you?"

"No," Raven said so softly, she knew Jade would have to strain to hear her. She wasn't sure why she was talking to the woman, why she felt like she could trust her after just meeting her, but she did. There was just something about her. "I couldn't. At first, it was because I wanted to protect my family, my kind, and our king. We try to keep our existence a secret from others, even other shifters. We live by different rules, rules coming from the king himself. He is the only one we answer to. Then, the more I learned about the General, I knew there was no way I could let him find out what I was. Could you imagine what would happen if he discovered dragons exist? He would go after them all. He would start a war that my king would be forced to finish, causing more death and destruction than you could ever imagine." Opening her eyes to look at Jade, she whispered, "If my king feels like our kind is being threatened, he will not hesitate to retaliate, and I'm afraid it won't matter who gets in the way, innocent or not. They will all die. It is best our existence is kept secret. At least, from the General and anyone who works for him."

"I understand," Jade murmured, smiling as she reached for the brush lying on the table next to her. "I can promise you, our pack will keep your secrets, Raven Dreher. We have many secrets among us. How about I tell you a few of my own while I comb your hair."

Raven eyed the brush in the other woman's hand, before nodding slowly. "It hurts," she admitted softly.

"I am sure everything does right now, but I also know how much you want those tangles out. I promise, I will be gentle, and I'll try to block the pain as much as possible."

"You can do that?" Raven asked in shocked surprise.

A wry grin crossed Jade's lips and she shrugged. "Not as well as my brother, Jinx, but I will do what I can."

Raven's eyes widened, and she looked at Jade closely.

"Jinx, is your brother?" She only knew one Jinx. The one who worked for the General.

"Yes. That's one of my secrets I am going to share with you." Taking a piece of the red-gold hair in her hand, Jade slowly pulled the strands apart, and then drew the brush down it as she started. "Jinx is my twin, stolen from my mother at birth."

"Your mother?'

"Angel is my mother."

Raven gasped, sitting up straighter, ignoring the pain that rushed through her at the movement. "The alpha's mate? Leader of the mercenary team?"

Jade's laughter filled the room as she slowly worked on Raven's hair. "Yes, the one and only."

For the next couple of hours, Jade told her tales of RARE and the White River Wolves, and their fight against the General, distracting Raven against any pain that was caused while she detangled her hair. When she finished, she laid the brush aside and took Raven's hands in her own. "I am so sorry for all that you have gone through, and for the part that my mate's father had in it."

Philip Perez, the man who had given the order for her to be taken in the first place, had started it all and sent Raven straight into hell.

"I would give anything to make it so that you didn't have to go through the misery you have this past year, Raven." Jade's eyes filled with tears as she whispered, "I feel your pain. It's like nothing I've ever felt before. It's never ending, always torturing you. I don't know how you stand it. I wish I could do something to help you."

Raven cupped the young woman's cheek, smiling

gently, "You already have, my new friend. You've given me hope."

"I have?"

"You faced the General, were his prisoner for twenty years, and look at you now. You are thriving in a new environment with family, friends, your pack. If you can do it, that gives me hope that I can, too."

"I wasn't tortured like you were," Jade whispered, bowing her head.

"There are several different kinds of torture, Jade. While mine was more physical, you still went through your own hell." Guiding those wide, emerald eyes back up to meet hers, Raven smiled gently. "Thank you so much for sharing your story with me. I know it was hard, but you have managed to give me so much more than you realize today."

"I have?"

"Along with hope, I now have the will to fight again. To push back the pain that haunts me and rise above it all. To survive. You did that for me, Jade. Thank you."

A brilliant smile crossed Jade's lips, lighting up her eyes. "You're welcome."

"Now," Raven said, letting her hand drop as she once again leaned back against the pillows. "Let's see how you did with my hair, shall we?"

Jade giggled, nodding her head in excitement. "I think you are going to like it!" Rising, she rushed from the room, but was back within moments, a small mirror in her hand. "You look beautiful, Raven. I think Jaxson is going to love it."

"Really?" Raven accepted the mirror Jade handed her, and hesitantly held it up in front of her. Amber eyes stared back at her. Her skin was pale from being away from the sun for so long, her lips a light pink, dry and chapped, but better than they had been just a couple of days ago. Those lips parted slightly as Raven stared in awe at the long mane of hair that now flowed in soft waves over her shoulders. Tears gathered in her eyes, but she refused to let them fall. With a shaky hand, she touched her hair, a soft smile covering her lips as she felt the silky smoothness. Lowering the mirror, she looked over at her new friend. "Thank you so much, Jade. You don't know how much this means to me."

Jade ducked her head shyly, her cheeks turning slightly pink. "I'm glad I could help."

The woman was a contradiction. So strong and giving, but also slightly unsure of herself. "If only there was something we could do about all of my scars," Raven said with a sigh.

"Scars?"

"I never really thought about it before, but I saw them when I was in the shower earlier." Sliding the covers down, Raven showed her one of her legs. "The scientists did a lot of experiments on me to try to figure out what kind of shifter I was. I think some of them really enjoyed it. I could smell their excitement." Raven slowly traced over one of the deep scars on her lower thigh, sighing before she slowly pulled the blanket back up. "What will Jaxson think?"

"He will think they are badges of courage," Jade said confidently, and Raven scented the truth in her words. "He is lucky to have you as his mate."

12

J axson slipped into the hospital room, shutting the door quietly behind him. He lifted a hand to Jade, but then his mind went blank when his gaze settled on his mate. Her eyes were closed, and she seemed to be sleeping peacefully, something she hadn't done since they arrived at the compound. She was so beautiful it made his heart hurt.

"She's been asleep for the past hour," Jade said softly. "I'm afraid to leave."

His gaze flew back to Jade, and he quickly crossed the room when he saw how pale she was. Small beads of sweat stood out on her forehead, and he could see she was in pain. "Jade, what are you doing?"

"I didn't want her to have to hurt anymore. I've been blocking the pain as much as I can, but it's going to come back full force when I leave," she confessed.

"You feel what she's been feeling?" he asked, knowing that wasn't good.

"Yes. I can't take her pain from her. I can't make her

better. I can just block it for a while. I wanted her to get some rest. All the suffering she's been through, she deserves it."

Jaxson swore softly, knowing there was going to be hell to pay when Jade's mate got there. Then he thought about his own mate feeling that pain again, and he had to fight back the loud roar that wanted to break free.

"I can't do this much longer," Jade admitted quietly, her breathing becoming ragged. "I am so sorry."

"Don't be," he told her gruffly. "You've given Raven a small respite. It will help her more than you realize."

Reaching out, he connected with Trace, including Angel on the telepathic link, knowing he might need her help to keep the panther calm. *Trace, I need you at the hospital right away. I just got here and found out your mate's been blocking Raven's pain. She's feeling it herself, and she's going to need you to get her home.*

Dammit! Trace snarled. *Why the hell would she do that?*

Because that's who my daughter is, Angel said. *You can't change her any more than I can, and you wouldn't want to.*

Fuck. I'm on my way.

Me, too, Angel said, severing the link.

"Your mate is on his way," Jaxson said, before glancing back over at Raven. She looked… happy. His jaw clenched tightly when he realized that look would be replaced by one of pain again soon, and he had to hold back a growl of anger.

Jade leaned her head back against the chair, her eyes closed, her hand clutching the arm rests tightly. "Thank you."

Moving around to the right side of the bed, Jaxson removed his boots, and then his weapons, setting them on the small table next to where Raven lay. Pulling back the covers, he slid in next to her and wrapped his arms around her, holding her close. Kissing her gently on the forehead, he smiled when she opened her eyes to look at him.

"No, thank you, Jade," he said quietly.

He heard the door open, but didn't take his gaze from his mate's.

"Jade, you've done all you can for now," Angel's voice was full of pride, but also sadness. "I am so proud of you, Daughter, but you need to let Raven bear her own pain again."

"But she hurts so much," Jade rasped, tears in her voice. "How does she do this? Feel this agony, every single day? How can anyone live with it?"

Jaxson was aware the moment Trace entered the room, low growls of anger coming from his chest. "You will break away now, my mate," he demanded.

"What's going on?" Dax demanded, stalking into the room, Sable and Rubi right behind him. "Is Raven okay?"

"I'm fine," Raven said softly, gently tracing Jaxson's features with her fingers. "Better than I have been in a long time." She kissed him softly, before turning to look at Jade.

"You are so strong, my friend. Thank you for blocking my pain enough so that I could get some sleep, but it's time to give it back to me."

"I don't want to," Jade whispered, moaning softly when Trace picked her up gently, and then sat down in the chair with her in his lap.

"You have to," Raven said, a small smile tilting up the corners of her lips. "You don't know how much it means to me that you are willing to shoulder the pain for me, but I've been handling it for the past year. I will be fine."

"No one should suffer like you do," Jade argued, small shudders racking her body as she fought to keep blocking the pain.

"You're just prolonging it, Jade," Angel said quietly. "You know you can't keep this up indefinitely."

"No, but I can just for a little longer."

Angel knelt beside her daughter, placing a hand on her arm. "Jade, I would take Raven's pain if I could. Any one of us would. But we can't. We don't have that ability. You have to give it back to her."

Jade looked over at Raven, shaking her head as she cried in despair. "I don't want you to feel this again."

"It will be fine," Raven promised, reaching out a hand to her. "I can handle it."

Tears tracked down Jade's cheeks as she grasped Raven's hand. She stared at her for a long moment, a loud moan tearing from her throat before she let go. "I am so sorry, Raven. So very sorry."

Jaxson knew the moment the full force of pain hit Raven again. Her back arched up off the bed, and a silent scream stuck in her throat, but no sound escaped. He held her close, whispering to her, unsure what he said. His heart clenched at the sight of his beautiful mate in so much agony, but there wasn't a damn thing he could do about it.

"God, Raven!" Jade cried, clutching her hand tightly. "Let me try to block it again."

"No!" Trace yelled. "You will not, Jade!"

"No," Raven rasped, burying her face in Jaxson's neck. "Listen to him, Jade. I'll be fine. I just need a minute."

"Oh, Raven," Rubi whispered, her voice trembling, "what can we do to help?"

"There isn't anything you can do," Raven gasped, holding her body stiffly against Jaxson's. He stared down into her eyes, swearing he could hear her soul crying out in misery.

"Maybe I can help."

He heard the soft voice but didn't recognize it. Holding Raven close, he turned to see a small woman with long brown hair that hung past her waist and chocolate brown eyes that seemed to see deep inside him standing in the open doorway. He inhaled, catching the scent of bear, and his brow furrowed.

"Alanna, no, we can't ask that of you," Angel said, moving toward the woman. "It's very sweet of you to offer, but we won't take advantage of your gifts."

Alanna Miller. The bear Chase's team rescued not too long ago. He'd forgotten all about her and her friend Fallon, who recently became a part of their pack. He wasn't aware that she had any gifts.

"You didn't ask anything of me," she said, walking passed Angel to the bed. "I want to help."

She was so small, but the power flowing from her wasn't. How had he not noticed that before?

"Alanna…"

Alanna ignored Angel, smiling down at Raven. "I can feel your pain, dragoness. Will you allow me to help?"

RAVEN STARED at the beautiful woman, wanting nothing

more than to accept her help, but she couldn't. Not if it meant it could hurt her.

"I don't want you to feel this," Raven whispered, laying her head weakly on Jaxson's shoulder.

"You don't have to worry about that," Alanna promised, running a hand gently down Raven's hair.

"It won't hurt you?"

"Not the way it does you."

"What's going on here?" Chase demanded, walking into the room

Alanna turned to smile at him, her hand resting lightly on Raven's shoulder. "Alpha, you are just in time."

"In time for what?" he growled, his hands going to his hips as he glared around the room.

"In time for me to help ease Raven of her pain," Alanna replied, sitting on the side of the bed and placing her other hand lightly on Raven's stomach. "I will need help back to my apartment after I'm finished, please."

"No!" Raven said, trying to pull away. "You said it wouldn't hurt you!"

"I said it wouldn't hurt me like it is hurting you," Alanna corrected, a gentle smile curving her lips. "There is always some pain in what I do, and I will feel very tired, but I will not suffer the way you are."

"You hurt when you took my pain?" Chase asked, a small hitch in his voice.

"A little." Alanna shrugged. "It is part of my gift. Now, let's begin, shall we?"

Raven looked over at Chase, unsure what to say. She didn't want this kind, caring woman to hurt, but the bear didn't seem willing to take no for an answer. When Chase nodded once, Raven's eyes went to Jaxson.

"I would appreciate any help you can give my mate," Jaxson told Alanna, his eyes never leaving Raven's. "I will be in your debt."

"There is no reason for that, wolf," Alanna replied. "Get comfortable, this could take a while."

Jaxson leaned back against the pillows, and Raven snuggled into his arms, fighting the tears that wanted to fall at the excruciating pain the movement caused. "Are you sure?" she asked one last time, giving the bear one more out.

Alanna closed her eyes and nodded. "Hush, dragoness, let me help you."

Raven immediately felt the power that began to flow in her. It was as if something ignited within her, flowing through her, and everywhere it touched, she became free of pain. She clutched tightly to Jaxson's shirt, crying out when she felt one of the worst areas in her stomach tighten in agony, and then seem to pulse as the pain slowly ebbed away.

"What is it? What's happening?" Jaxson demanded.

Tears leaked from Raven's eyes, and she tilted her head up to look at him. "It's working."

"There is always pain in healing," Alanna said, a low moan escaping as she moved her hands, one settling on Raven's chest above her heart and the other on her thigh. "You poor woman. The things you've been through. Let you live free of all of your pain and suffering. You deserve it. I will allow no less."

Raven cried out again as Alanna's power met a spot in her chest, where she had thought the scientists were literally going to carve out her heart one day. "Hurts!"

"Yes, I can feel it, dragoness. I promise, it won't much

longer." True to her word, soon the pain seemed to come to a head, and then ebb away again, just as it had before. "We're almost done," Alanna whispered, moving her hands one more time. "I'm sorry this is taking so long. You have been through so much. I need to make sure you are completely healed, and that no more pain will bother you."

It took fifteen more minutes, but finally, Alanna stepped back, swaying slightly on her feet. "There. It is done."

Raven lay glued to Jaxson, afraid to move. She was so tired, and it was a struggle to open her eyes, but she felt better. Her body ached slightly, but the unbearable pain was gone. How the hell had Alanna done that?

"She will need a lot of rest for the next few hours. I've never encountered anything like her pain before."

"Thank you so much," Jaxson said gruffly. Raven felt him kiss the top of her head gently. "You ever need anything, Alanna, you call me."

"Me, too," Dax growled. "Anything. I can't thank you enough for what you've done for my sister."

"Thank you, but as I said before, there is no need. I'm just glad I could help. She is definitely worthy of it."

"Let's get you back to your apartment," Chase said quietly. "You look like you are about to fall over."

Alanna laughed softly. "I won't deny it. This healing took a lot out of me." Raven felt the woman place a gentle hand on her arm as she said, "Sleep, dragoness. I will be back to see you in a few days."

Raven tried to thank her, she really did, but she could form no words. Exhaustion beat at her, and slowly she succumbed to it, feeling safe in her mate's arms.

13

J axson woke up to hands trailing over his chest and down lower, to rest on his lower stomach. Slowly, they inched his shirt up, and then he bit back a groan as they slid sensuously over his skin. "Raven." He breathed her name, loving the way she was touching him, needing more.

"Jaxson," she murmured, sliding his shirt up, urging him to take it all the way off. "Please, I need to touch you."

Groaning, Jaxson slipped it off, and then let his hands slide down over her sides, grasping the hem of the hospital gown and sliding it up. He paused, having the presence of mind to ask, "Am I hurting you?" He wanted to touch her, to feel her silky skin, but not if he was going to cause her pain.

Ignoring his question, she trailed kisses over his chest, her tongue circling his nipple, before she gently bit down on it, her other hand sliding down to cup his growing erection.

"Fuck! Raven!"

He felt her grin against his skin, and then she looked up at him, her amber eyes glowing, reminding him of a bright gem. "No, you aren't hurting me. The pain is gone, Jaxson. All of it." There was happiness in her voice, and a deep contentment that he hadn't heard from her before.

"I'm glad." He slid his hand into her thick hair, loving the way the reds and golds swirled together. She smiled at him, a pink blush settling in her cheeks. "You are so beautiful, Raven."

The brightness of her eyes seemed to dim slightly, and she shook her head. "Maybe I used to be, but I'm not anymore. Jaxson, I have so many scars now. They may fade, but they will never go away."

"You think I care about that?" Jaxson asked, leaning in to touch his lips to hers, before slowly trailing kisses from her mouth down her neck, to her shoulder. "I see who you are, Raven, deep inside. Kind, caring, loving. Those are the things I care about. Who you are deep down, not what you look like." Reaching behind her, he undid the tie to the gown, and then slid it down her shoulders. "We all have scars. I have acquired a few of my own over the years. Does that matter to you?"

"Of course not."

He raised his head to look at her, "Then, why would you think it would matter to me?"

"I guess I wasn't thinking," she whispered.

"Well, I don't want you to think about anything right now," he said, lowering his head to capture one of her nipples in his mouth. He swirled his tongue around it, before sucking on it, then biting it gently. When she cried out, he pulled back to say, "All I want you doing right now is feeling. I want you to remember what it's like to feel pleasure instead of pain."

"Jaxson!" she gasped, clutching at his shoulders, moaning as she arched into him.

Grinning, he lowered his head again, playing with her nipple. Sucking, nibbling, biting down gently. As he did, he slipped the gown off, leaving her body bare for him to explore. Rising up on all fours, he grinned at her, loving the way her head was flung back, her chest heaving as she tried to catch her breath. Slowly, he licked his way down her body, groaning when she slipped her fingers into his hair, clutching it tightly as she encouraged him to go lower.

"Please, Jaxson, I want your mouth on me."

If his dick wasn't hard enough before, it was rock hard now. His woman knew what she wanted, and she wasn't shy about asking for it. "I got you, baby," he promised, licking his way over her navel, and then lower to where she really wanted him. Spreading her legs, his tongue flicked out, playing with the small bud, and Raven moaned, raising her hips to push into him. He fucking loved it.

"Jaxson, I need more!"

Groaning, he tasted her, sinking his tongue into her wetness, a low growl slipping free when the flavor of her coated his tongue. The small noises she made as she clutched his hair tightly while moving her hips and begging him for more drove him wild. Licking up her folds, he slid a finger deep inside of her, and then flicked her clit with his tongue.

"Oh, God, Jaxson! Like that!"

Adding another finger, he began to slide them in and

out of her, moving his tongue faster. After a moment, he felt her stiffen, and then a scream left her lips as she came, pulsing against his fingers. He continued to lick her, lapping up her juices until she was spent, and then he slowly slid back up her body and held her close.

When she began to slide her hand down toward his aching cock, he captured it in his and raised it to kiss her knuckles. "Not yet."

"But you didn't get…"

"I have everything I need right here," he promised, holding her body close to his, loving the way their chests felt pressed together, skin against skin. When she didn't respond, he tilted her head up to meet his gaze. "Trust me, baby, I want you so much right now I ache. I want to feel your lips on my cock. I want to be deep inside of you. I want to sink my teeth in your skin and claim the fuck out of you. I want all of it. But, not here. Not in a hospital bed."

"Oh!" Raven's cheeks darkened a deep red, and she glanced toward the door. "I wasn't thinking. Do you think they heard?"

Jaxson burst out laughing, reaching down to pull the blanket over her. "Honey, I think the entire White River Wolves compound heard you." When she covered her face with her hands, Jaxson pulled them away and grinned. "I fucking loved it. Now, every male in this pack will know you are mine."

Raven returned his grin, ducking her head before saying. "Good. I want them to."

"What news do you have for me?" the General demanded, glaring at the two imbeciles in front of him.

"They're back at the White River Wolves compound," one of them said, and the General grinned in satisfaction when he saw the man was literally shaking in his boots. Good. He should be, because he fucked up. And he was about to pay the price.

"And the woman?"

"We haven't seen her, but we assume they have her with them."

"You assume?" the General thundered, ignoring the throbbing pain in his throat. "You didn't actually see her?"

"Well, no, but where else would she be?'

"Where else, indeed?" He'd had enough of both of them. They were the reason one of his most prized possessions was missing in the first place. It had been their job to remove her from the facility in D.C. when the alarm sounded; a job they neglected to do. Instead, they'd ran like the cowards they were.

Glancing over at Ebony, he said, "I'm done with them."

She nodded, knowing what he wanted. He heard their protests as he turned and walked away. He didn't listen. They'd failed him. Death was their punishment.

Two shots rang out, one right after the other, and soon his daughter was walking beside him.

"We need to keep moving, General," she said as she slid her gun back into the holster at her hip. "This facility doesn't have the safeguards some of the others do."

"I have some decisions to make first," he replied, making his way to the back of the building to the room he was using as his office for now.

"Yes, Father."

"When is Jinx expected to arrive?"

"Soon."

"I'm here." The General almost jumped at the sound of the assassin's voice as he entered his office, his gaze going to where Jinx stood by the one window in the room. The man was fucking scary, even to him.

"You didn't check in."

Jinx turned to him, a sardonic look on his face. "When do I ever check in, General? I do the job you send me to do, then I come back."

It was the truth. The cocky bastard never checked in until he saw the General again, but he always got the job done.

"They are dead?"

"Did you send me to kill them?"

The General stiffened, rage filling him at the man's

condescending attitude. If he didn't need the little bastard, he would have gotten rid of him years ago.

"They are gone," Jinx confirmed, his gaze going back to the window and beyond.

"And what did you find in D.C. when you went back?"

"There were no bodies."

"None?"

"None."

That's what he'd suspected after watching what there was of the video in the basement before the building blew. That meant Raven was still alive, as were all the others. Damn. He'd been hoping to get at least a couple of the bastards. "That's disappointing."

Jinx shrugged. "It is what it is."

"I have a job for you, Jinx."

Jinx moved from the window, leaning his back up against the wall next to it, crossing his arms over his chest. "Go on."

"I lost something in D.C., and I want it back." When Jinx raised an eyebrow, but didn't respond, he went on, "A shifter."

Jinx frowned. "We didn't have any shifters in the facility. You moved them all before your accident."

Accident. The General's hands clenched tightly into fists, the pain in his neck now clawing at him. There had been no accident. Chase Montgomery had tried to tear his throat out and had almost succeeded. For that, the man would die someday. Soon.

"No, he didn't," Ebony said, sitting in one of the chairs in front of the desk, crossing one leg over the other. "He kept one locked up like an animal in the basement."

"They are all fucking animals," the General snarled, rounding the desk to sit in his own chair.

"Really?" Jinx asked, raising an eyebrow, his face a blank mask.

"Really," the General snarled, slamming his fist into the desk, forgetting for a moment that Jinx was one of those animals.

"What are my orders, General?" Jinx asked, his voice low and controlled.

"You will go to the White River Wolves compound, and you will bring back my acquisition that they stole." Turning to a monitor, the General pulled up the last video feed he had of the woman. "This is Raven," he said, pointing to the screen. "She's a shifter, but we haven't been able to determine what kind. I've had her for a year, and we were getting close to breaking her, but then the D.C. facility was raided and she was stolen. I want her back."

"You want me to infiltrate the White River Wolves compound, find her, and bring her back here?"

"Yes, unless you think you can't complete the mission for some reason? If not, I can give it to someone who can."

"I'll do it for you, General," Ebony purred. "Sounds like fun."

"Jinx?"

"I'll handle it."

"Good. I will expect to hear from you within the week. That will be all."

Jinx strode from the room without another word, shutting the door behind him on his way out.

Sitting back in his chair, the General rested his elbows

on the chair arms and steepled his fingers. "Now, let's discuss the Amber issue."

JINX PAUSED in the hallway when he heard Amber's name, wondering what kind of trouble the woman had gotten herself into now. Her bleeding heart was going to get her killed someday if she wasn't careful.

"I've placed her somewhere no one will find her, not that anyone will look," Ebony said snidely.

"I don't want her killed...yet. She may still be useful to us."

"Yes, Father."

"That being said, she doesn't need to be too comfortable, either."

"Oh, trust me, she isn't anywhere near comfortable."

Jinx stifled a low growl and he clenched his hands tightly into fists. Amber was in trouble, and there wasn't a damn thing he could do about it right now. He had his orders, and he needed to at least act like he was going to follow through with them.

"What about Vixen?"

"Oh, that bitch is definitely up to something." Ebony's voice was hard, like ice. "I haven't figured out what yet, but I will."

"Don't waste your time," the General said, and Jinx heard him slide his chair back. "She won't be a problem to us for much longer."

"And if things don't work out the way you plan?"

"Then, I will let you take care of it."

"Yes, General."

Jinx had heard enough. He needed to get the hell out of there before the General's viper of a daughter opened the door. Baring his teeth, he stalked down the hall, careful not to make a sound. He needed to get to the White River Wolves compound first. He would figure out what to do about Raven on the way. Then, he was going hunting for Amber.

15

"This is where we will live?" Raven asked softly, her eyes roaming over the living room of the apartment before she wandered into the kitchen. It was after eight at night, but she had hounded the doctor enough that she'd finally allowed her to leave the hospital. Even though Raven wasn't hurting anymore, Doc Josie wanted to monitor her to make sure everything healed correctly. While the bear had managed to make all of the pain go away, whatever she'd done hadn't fully healed all of Raven's wounds. Alanna and her gifts were a mystery to her, but Raven would be forever thankful for the woman.

"I have a place in Denver, but have been staying here most of the time these past few months," Jaxson told her. "It's better that we are all close in case the General tries anything."

That explained why the apartment was so bare. It had all the necessities—furniture, a television mounted to the wall, a kitchen table and chairs—but there were no personal effects. "So, we will be staying here for now?"

"Actually, I was thinking we would move in here permanently, if it's okay with you," Jaxson said, holding out a hand to her. "Your brother and his mate are just down the hall, and Rubi is in this building, too. I thought you might want to be close to them."

"Yes, please," she whispered, her heart filling with joy at the thought of living near her family. "I've missed them so much."

"Raven," Jaxson paused, resting his forehead against hers. "Once this is all over with the General and it's safe, I will live wherever you want. Here, the place you used to call home, I don't care."

"What about RARE and your pack?" Raven whispered, her hands going to his chest.

"They are my family, but you are my life."

A slow smile spread across her face as she looked into his eyes. "My home is with you, wherever that may be, but I am thinking that is here, my wolf. My sister and brother are here, you're here, that's all I need."

As she watched, his eyes darkened, his wolf showing through, and there was a low growl as his fangs appeared. "I don't want to wait anymore, Raven."

She knew what he meant, and she was in full agreement. "Then don't," she breathed, licking her lips in anticipation. His gaze dropped to where her tongue had snuck out and he groaned, closing the distance between them to capture her mouth with his.

Jaxson lifted her into his arms, and she felt as if she were floating as he made his way down the hall, kicking open a door at the end. Lifting his head, he smiled, his eyes going to the room behind her. "I hope you like it."

Following his gaze, Raven gasped in surprise, her

hands clutching tightly to Jaxson's shirt as her eyes misted over. "You did all of this for me?"

"You deserve the best," he whispered, bending his head to gently rub his cheek against hers.

The room was aglow in a soft light, lit by the candles in the room. There were so many of them. Light pink rose petals were scattered across the floor leading to the large king-sized bed, that was covered with darker red ones. "It's so beautiful," Raven murmured in awe.

"You're beautiful," Jaxson said, closing the door behind them and crossing the room to lay her gently on the bed. "I am so lucky to have found you, Raven. I will spend my entire life loving you, cherishing you the way you should be cherished."

Raven's bottom lip trembled as she stared up at the man who would be hers for all time. She was the lucky one. When she was young, she'd dreamed about the day she would someday find her mate. In her dreams, he had always been a fearless dragon, but she wouldn't trade her wolf for anything. He was everything she'd ever wanted; kind, considerate, caring, protective, loyal. And he was hers. "Jaxson, please."

"Please what?" he growled playfully, as he removed his shirt, then sat down on the bed to untie his boots. She waited until he had them off before she responded.

"Bite me."

Jaxson froze, a shudder going through his broad shoulders before he slowly rose. Turning, his hands fisted at his sides, he growled, "Be sure, baby. There's no going back once I claim you."

"I'm sure." Her heart pounded in anticipation as she watched his hands go to his jeans. She was more than sure. He undid the button, slid the zipper down, and his cock sprang free. Her mouth watered at the sight, and she rose to her knees, making her way over to him. Grasping the sides of his jeans, she shoved them down, waiting impatiently for him to kick them off. "No underwear?"

"Don't like the way they feel."

Raven reached out and trailed her fingers up his cock, loving the way the skin felt velvety soft over the hard length. When a drop of pre-cum leaked out, she spread it over the tip with her thumb. Moaning, she slid from the bed so she was kneeling in front of him, and leaned in close, inhaling his scent.

"Fuck, Raven, you put your mouth on me, I don't know if I will survive."

"You better," she whispered, "because I want to feel you deep inside me when you sink your fangs in me and claim me. But first, I need to see what you taste like." Not waiting for a response, she leaned in and licked the tip of his dick, moaning as her eyes closed in passion, and then she sucked him deep.

"Raven!"

Cupping his balls in one hand, she wrapped her other hand around the lower part of his cock, moving it up and down, matching the motion of her mouth. Low growls of pure pleasure slipped from her throat and she began to move faster.

"Raven! Shit, I'm going to come."

Hell yeah, she wanted him to. The growls built up, louder and louder, her entire body on fire.

Suddenly, Jaxson pulled free from her mouth. Before she could argue, he helped her to her feet and turned her around. "I'm not coming in your mouth, mate. I'm making you mine."

"Oh!" she gasped, when he bent her over the side of the bed and spread her legs. Then he was there, deep inside her, filling her slowly. "Jaxson!" It felt so good, so right.

"Baby, you're fucking tight."

"More!" she begged, arching back into him. "I need to feel you, Jaxson."

"I want to be gentle," he growled. "I'm trying so hard not to take you the way I want to. You deserve better."

"Screw gentle," she snarled, pushing back against him. "I'm not going to break, Jaxson. What I deserve is my mate."

Gripping her hips firmly, Jaxson held her still for a moment. "Is this what you want?" he growled, before he thrust deep inside her. Pulling out, he slammed back in again. "Like this?"

"Yes!" she cried, her claws lengthening, tearing holes in the sheets. "Make me feel alive, Jaxson! Make me yours!"

A loud roar tore from his chest and Jaxson began to move faster, thrusting into her again and again. "Mine!" he snarled, lowering his head and covering her shoulder with his teeth.

"Yes! Yours!" Raven felt the fire before she saw it, the flames moving along her arms and over her body, and knew it would transfer to Jaxson as well. It wouldn't hurt him, though. A dragon's fire never hurt their mate. Her body shook with desire, so close to exploding. "Jaxson, please!"

He bit down, and she flew apart, screaming his name as she came. She felt him stiffen, and then he was pulsing inside her, low growls emitting from around where his teeth dug into her shoulder. "Mine. Mine."

She let him hold her still for a moment longer, and then she growled, "My turn."

Sliding him out of her, she turned and lay on the bed, opening her arms to him. He didn't hesitate, covering her with his body, and slipping back into her heat. Opening her mouth wide, Raven hovered over his shoulder for a second, and then sank her fangs deep. Jaxson yelled her name and she felt him jerking inside her again. Then, their souls merged as one, bringing with it a peace that she'd never known before.

JAXSON HELD RAVEN CLOSE, her head on his chest, as he stroked his hand gently over the silky skin on her back. He couldn't believe he'd found her. His mate. He had RARE and his pack, and they were his family, but now, he had so much more. He had someone to come home to, to love and to spend the rest of his life with. It made him happier than he'd ever been, but it also terrified him. What if he couldn't protect her from all of the evil in the world? There was so much of it.

"Jaxson, where did you go?" Raven whispered, tilting her head up to look at him.

Leaning down, he placed a kiss on the tip of her nose. "I'm right here, baby."

Kissing his chest, she smiled, "You know what I meant."

He did, but he was having a hard time trying to figure

out how to respond. He hadn't talked about that part of his life in so long, he wasn't even sure where to start.

"Jaxson?"

Sighing, he pulled her close and closed his eyes. "I was thinking about my family," he admitted.

"Family?"

"Yeah." It had all happened years ago, but the thought of it still crushed him. He was silent for several minutes before he finally said, "I lost my family fifty-three years ago. My parents, my sister, my brother. All of them."

"What happened?"

"Our alpha died, and a new one took over," Jaxson's arms tightened around her as he thought back to a time he wanted to forget. "He was cruel. A real son of a bitch." He swallowed hard before continuing, "I was in the military and away on tour in another country. I knew we had a new alpha, but I didn't know everything that was going on until I got back." Raven raised up and placed a soft kiss on his chin, then snuggled up closer to him. "I missed my family so much. We were very close, which must be why they kept what was happening from me. They knew I would be on the first plane back and there would be hell to pay." He gritted his teeth, taking a deep breath before he continued, "I got home late one night. I hadn't talked to anyone in my family in over a month because where I was, the mission I was on, made it impossible. But I was home for good. My time with the military was up, and I'd decided not to re-enlist. I wanted to surprise them." Pain engulfing him at the thought of what he'd come home to, he rasped, "When I walked into my parents' house, there was blood everywhere. It was old, but it was theirs. My dad's, mom's, Connel's, and Moon's. I went straight to the alpha's house and confronted him. He told me my family had been attacked by a rogue wolf pack. None of them made it."

"Oh, Jaxson."

Gritting his teeth, he ground out, "It was a lie. I smelled it on the fucker, but had no grounds to go after him. So, instead I dug. I dug as deep as I could, discovering things that tore me apart. I found out the alpha had wanted my sister. My fourteen-year-old sister, Raven. When my parents refused, he had them murdered. When my brother and sister tried to intervene, they died, too."

"What did you do?"

He stiffened, and then rasped, "I killed them all. Every last motherfucker who had a part in my family's death died. And then, I left my pack, a pack I had loved before that bastard took it over, and never went back. I don't regret it. None of it."

"Good," Raven whispered, her hand going up to slide into his hair. She was quiet for a moment, and then said, "You make me so damn proud to be your mate, Jaxson."

He couldn't believe this woman was his. Wondering how he had gotten so lucky, he hauled her up so she straddled his waist and growled, "Show me."

16

Jaxson tugged Raven close for another kiss, running a hand down her back. "I'll be back as soon as I can," he promised. He hated leaving her even for a minute, but he was late for a meeting with Angel and the team.

Raven clung to him, pressing tightly against his body. He groaned, moving his hands down to cup her ass and pull her up into his thickening erection. He couldn't get enough of the woman.

"Get a room, you two," Sable teased, slipping past them in the hallway.

"Please do," Dax growled, right behind her. "I don't want to watch my sister being felt up in the halls where I live."

Raven giggled, standing on her tip toes to kiss Jaxson on the cheek. "Like we don't all know what you and Sable were doing just a few minutes ago, big brother."

"In the privacy of our own bedroom," he groused,

shaking his head, but Jaxson saw his eyes were full of laughter.

"We won't be long, Sis," Rubi said, shutting her door behind her as she joined Dax and Sable at the end of the hall.

"Let's go, wolf!" Dax hollered, holding the door to the stairwell open for Sable and Rubi.

"You sure you're going to be okay?" Jaxson asked Raven, leaning down to rub his cheek against hers. "I hate leaving like this."

"I'll be just fine," Raven said, pushing him away with a laugh. "I'm going to go check on Alanna. Rubi told me she's in this building, too. She shares a place on the main floor with her friend, Fallon."

"Okay, but you do not leave this building, understand?" He had a feeling the General wasn't done yet. Raven was too valuable to the bastard, even if he didn't fully understand why.

"I am only going to go talk to Alanna," Raven promised. "She's in apartment three on the first floor. If I'm not here when you get back, I'll be there."

Jaxson wrapped his arms around her, burying his face in her hair. "I'm sorry if I'm being an overbearing ass, Raven. I just… I can't lose you."

"You aren't going to lose me," Raven murmured, kissing his neck. "I'll be right here waiting for you."

Jaxson hugged her close for a long moment before sighing and giving her one last kiss. "Be back soon, sweet mate."

A brilliant smile lit up her face as she stepped back, waving to her brother, who still waited at the end of the hall. "Take care of my man, Dax, or I'm going to kick your ass!"

Dax threw his head back and laughed, "Don't you worry, little sister. I'll take care of your pup."

Jaxson stalked down the hall, stopping just long enough to slam a fist in the dragon's ribs before sliding past him into the stairwell. Fighting the urge to glance back one last time to see if his beautiful mate still watched him go, he gave in and glanced back, his heart expanding when she waved to him, blowing him a kiss. This fucking meeting better be quick.

———

RAVEN KNOCKED LIGHTLY on Alanna's apartment door, glancing down the hall when the outside door opened and a woman walked in, a small child in her arms. She smiled at Raven, saying hello shyly, before slipping through the stairwell door out of sight.

Knocking again, Raven waited impatiently for the bear to answer. She could hear noise in the apartment, knew someone was there, but for some reason they weren't opening the door.

"Alanna, it's Raven." When there was no reply, she called, "Please let me in, Alanna. I just want to check on you."

She sensed a presence on the other side of the door, and then it was opened by a tall woman with short, black hair that was a bright pink color on the tips. Her dark grey eyes glanced behind Raven furtively, and then she opened the door wider to let Raven in, shutting it quickly behind her.

"Alanna's resting," she said softly, motioning toward the kitchen. "I'm Fallon, her friend and roommate. Would you like some coffee?"

Raven could smell the other woman's apprehension, but was confused as to why. "No, thank you." Holding out a hand, Raven said, "I'm Raven."

"I know who you are." Sighing, Fallon ignored her outstretched hand and motioned to the kitchen again. "Please, come in and have a seat. I need some coffee, even if you don't."

Raven frowned, but walked into the kitchen and sat at the table. "Is everything all right?" she asked tentatively. She waited impatiently until the woman got her coffee and sat down across from her before asking again, "Is Alanna okay?"

"No, she's not." Fallon took a deep breath, before saying, "Anytime Alanna uses her healing abilities, this happens."

"What?"

"She doesn't want anyone to know." Fallon stared down into her cup, holding it between both hands. "What she does, helping people when she can, is important to her. She doesn't want them to know what it does to her. The toll it takes on her."

"Tell me."

Fallon lifted her exhausted gaze to meet Raven's, and she whispered, "The repercussions of using her gifts doesn't normally set in until an hour or so later, but when it does, she needs to be somewhere safe. Her body becomes leaden. She can't move, can't eat. It's a fight to even get liquids down her."

"Is she in pain?" Raven asked in horror, even though she was afraid she already knew the answer.

"When she removes someone's pain like she did yours, she can't help but feel it herself. It isn't the same as what you felt, not to the same extent, but yes, she is in pain," Fallon explained. "She told me once that it is as if she is absorbing your pain, but as she is taking it from your body, only bits and pieces of it are actually getting into hers." Fallon shrugged helplessly. "I'm sorry, I'm not very good at this. Before Alanna, I never even knew these kinds of gifts existed. I still don't understand hers. All I know, is that when she does something like this, when she helps someone in need, it's a struggle for her afterwards."

"I am so sorry," Raven whispered, regret filling her. "If I had known, there is no way I would have allowed her to heal me."

"Which is why she never says anything," Fallon murmured, her gaze going back to her cup. "Alanna feels this driving need to help everyone in pain. She calls it a gift, I call it a curse."

"You are afraid it's going to kill her someday."

Fallon raised her head and gazed at Raven solemnly. "She's been in her bed since she helped you, Raven. This is the worst I've ever seen her. Alanna is kind, gentle, but has a backbone of steel. I'm afraid she is going to come across someone someday she feels the need to heal, and it is going to break her. Because no matter what I say, or what anyone else says, Alanna will do what she says is her calling. When she does, she will be lost to us."

"No," Raven protested, rising to her feet. "I won't allow it."

"You won't be able to stop her."

"Watch me," Raven growled, stalking from the kitchen and following Alanna's scent to her bedroom. She knocked softly, before opening the door. What she saw inside made her stiffen, her hand tightening on the doorknob.

Alanna lay unmoving in her bed, her skin so pale it was almost as if it was translucent. There were dark shadows under her eyes, and her cheeks were hollow, her body appearing even smaller than Raven remembered. A tear escaped, sliding down her cheek as Raven realized this was her fault. The sweet bear was lying in that bed, suffering, because of her.

Crossing the room, Raven sat in a wooden chair that was beside the bed and covered Alanna's hand with hers. "Why?" she whispered, a tear escaping at the thought of what the little bear must be going through. "Why did you help me, knowing this would happen to you?"

Alanna's eyelids fluttered, and then Raven was staring into dark brown eyes. What shocked her was they were filled with warmth and compassion. "Because you have lived in agony for a very long time, dragoness. My suffering will go away in a matter of days. The pain will go away, as will the weakness, and I will be fine soon."

Swallowing hard, Raven reached out and gently stroked a piece of long, brunette hair away from Alanna's face. "Well, my friend, I will be here for you if you need me."

"There is no need."

"Yes, there is," Raven said, smiling gently. "You have done so much for me at great risk to yourself. I don't know how I will ever repay you."

"Your friendship is all I need," Alanna said softly as her eyes drifted slowly shut.

"You will always have that," Raven vowed.

17

Jinx stood high on a hill overlooking the White River Wolves compound. He'd been given orders, ones he had no intention of completing, but he knew he wasn't the only one the General would send. He had some tough decisions to make. He had vowed to end the General, stopping his reign of terror and bringing down his entire operation. He'd been cold as ice, letting no one get in the way of his final objective, until Angel and her team entered the picture. Yes, he had helped several captives in the past, had avoided kill orders when they were for innocent lives, relocating them with new names and identities so the General wouldn't find them, but not once did he endanger his final objective while doing it. Until now.

There was no way out of the predicament he found himself in now. He'd let his emotions get in the way, let himself feel for the first time in a long time, and it was too late. Raven was an innocent. She was mate to a member of RARE, which made her part of the White River Wolves pack now. His pack, if he accepted the open-ended invitation to join given to him by Chase Montgomery, his mother's mate. All he had to do was say yes. He wanted to more than anything. He was tired of being alone. He wanted to know what it was like to be a part of a family. To have friends. To find someone to love and have a mate of his own at home. Unfortunately, that wasn't going to happen. His time had come. He had a decision to make, his life or Raven's. To him, there really was no choice.

Movement caught his eye, and a cold grin settled on his features. No, there was no choice, but before he could follow through with what needed to be done, he had to dispense of the threat to the dragoness here at the compound. He welcomed the fight. And it would be a good one. The General hadn't pulled any punches. He'd sent one of his best assassins, as if he somehow knew Jinx would not follow through.

Jinx ran swiftly through the forest of trees, losing sight of the woman as she moved stealthily toward the center of the compound. That conniving son of a bitch was good. Sending this particular assassin after Raven the same time he sent Jinx. The General knew she was the only one who had a chance of besting Jinx on her own, and if she failed, then Jinx would rid him of what he considered a problem anyway, because he'd already stated that he didn't trust her. Vixen. This was going to be one hell of a fight.

The bitch was already in the middle of the compound before he caught up with her. Refusing to play the assassin game, slipping in and out of places without people seeing him, Jinx decided fuck it, and walked right down the middle of the street, shoulders back, head held high. Vixen was not going to get her prey today, no matter how hard she fought, and he was tired of sneaking around. Bring it out to the open, he thought. It wasn't like they were going to be able to keep what was about to happen quiet, anyway.

Holding one hand up when two female wolves glanced in his direction as he neared the park, he said, "Get those pups indoors. Now!"

"Jinx? What's going on?"

He heard his sister, but didn't acknowledge her except to say, "Get everyone out of here, Jade. It's not safe." Pulling his sword from its sheath, he stopped in the middle of the street and called out, "Vixen! I know you are here. Show yourself!"

The woman stepped from the shadows, twirling a sai in one hand as she sauntered toward him. The weapon was deadly — a dagger with two sharp prongs curving outward from the hilt. Vixen's weapon of choice, and she knew how to use it. "Jinx. Fancy meeting you here." She wore black leathers that fit her like a glove, a sleeveless black shirt, and black boots that went up to her knees. Her dark eyes glittered with excitement and malicious intent as they traced over him. "Although, I have to say I'm a little surprised."

Cocking an eyebrow, Jinx slowly began to move his wrist, bringing attention to the way his sword swirled around him. "Oh yeah? Why's that?"

"What the hell is going on here?" Chase Montgomery demanded, as he came out of the building to their right, stalking toward them, his face a mask of pure anger. He had every right to be mad as hell. They were endangering his pack, and no alpha would stand for that.

"Jinx? Who is this?"

Jinx ignored Angel, his full attention on the woman in front of him. He couldn't afford to avert his gaze. It would get him killed.

"Her name is Vixen," Steele said, moving up beside them. The whole fucking RARE team had come to join the party, along with many of the White River Wolves. At least, they were smart enough to stay back. "She's one of the General's assassins. A very dangerous one."

"Aren't they all dangerous?" someone asked.

"Not like Vixen." Steele told them. "She will tear your heart out and move on to the next target in the blink of an eye."

"What the fuck is she doing here?" Chase demanded, taking a step in their direction.

Steele stopped him, a hand on his arm. "You need to let my son handle this, Alpha. Trust me, he's the only one who can."

"Son?" Vixen asked, arching an eyebrow. "The General's pet has a daddy?" she said snidely.

Jinx didn't respond, slowly twirling his sword as he watched her move closer to him. He was aware of the crowd they were attracting, but his gaze narrowed on the woman in front of him. She was the one who really mattered. "You can't have her, Vixen."

"I have my orders."

"He's not getting her."

"I'm pretty sure you have the same orders I have, Jinx. Tell me, are you disobeying your master?"

"I have no master," he growled, baring his teeth, but refused to let her bait him.

"What are they talking about?" he heard someone ask.

"She's here for Raven, isn't she?" Rubi snarled. "She isn't getting her!"

"No," Jinx said, his voice low and deadly, "she isn't. I made a promise, and I fully intend to keep it."

No sooner had the words left his lips, then Vixen made her move. She was faster than he anticipated, and he almost didn't move quick enough, the sai missing him by mere inches. Feinting to the left, he brought his sword around in a circle, aiming for the sai she held, but she was already gone.

"You know this is pointless, Jinx," she said, pulling another sai from her boot. "The General wants his property back, and what the General wants, the General gets."

"My sister is not his fucking property!" Rubi snapped, making a move toward them. It distracted Jinx just enough that the next swipe Vixen made managed to slice through his forearm.

Steele wrapped his arm tightly around Rubi's waist and swung her around to drop her next to Dax, snarling, "You will keep her next to you so that she doesn't get my son killed! He cannot afford to have his attention divided."

"Awe," Vixen purred, her lips in a pout. "Did the big bad wolf get a boo boo? Would you like me to…"

Jinx struck, his sword lightning fast, drawing blood as it came away. When Vixen's eyes widened, her lips parting slightly in surprise, he muttered, "He's watching you, ya know?"

Her hands tightened on her sais as she crouched down low, one in front of her, one pointed to the ground. "Why would he do that?"

"Late check-ins."

Her eyes narrowed, and she growled, "Ebony. She's been creeping around my facility a lot lately."

"Yep."

"That bitch."

"She's not the only one."

Vixen flew at him, slicing and dicing when she got near. Jinx grunted as the blades bit into his skin, leaving deep cuts, and then she was gone. She thought she was safe, but he didn't waste any time. He was on her before she came to a complete stop, and then the fight was on. Soon, it was obvious they were pretty evenly matched, which shocked the hell out of him. He'd known she was good, but had no idea just how good. It was almost a struggle to keep up with her, a fight that drew blood on both sides, until she made one fatal mistake, and then he was on her, his sword to her throat.

"Do it," she snarled, blood flowing from several deep wounds, coating the ground she lay on. "That's why you're here, isn't it? To take me out for that son of a bitch? Fucking do it!"

He almost did. He was so close, but there was something in her eyes, something he couldn't look away from. Misery, suffering, turmoil, guilt. Suddenly, he knew. That mistake she made wasn't a mistake after all. She wanted to die.

"Please, Jinx," she rasped, realizing he knew the truth now. "I can't do this anymore. The killing, murdering, I just can't. I'm ready to leave this life."

As he stared at her, bleeding out on the ground, he realized that everything she was feeling right now was the same he felt. He was so fucking tired of it all. Slowly, he removed his sword from her throat and slid it in the scabbard at his back. His entire body ached, and he was covered with his blood, as well as hers. They were fighting a fight neither of them really wanted anything to do with.

Kneeling beside her, Jinx placed his palm on her forehead. Vixen tried to pull away, but she was too weak from the blood loss. Closing his eyes, he slipped inside her mind. It was utter chaos. She hated the life she led and was looking for a way out. He delved deeper and saw what he knew she didn't want him to see. The victims she saved. The ones she hid from the General. The children. There were so many children. They were the reason she had been late checking in. She was saving lives, way more than she was taking.

Slipping back out of her mind, Jinx met Vixen's eyes. She stared at him, her hand coming up to clutch at his wrist. "Now you know my secrets."

"Yes."

"You can't tell him," she rasped, her eyes fluttering as she fought to stay conscious. "He will find them and kill them all." When he didn't respond, she cried, "You should have just killed me, dammit! I could have taken my secrets to the grave."

She began to shiver, her body going into shock, and Jinx knew he couldn't let her die. Taking her hand in his, he held it to his heart as he vowed, "I will never tell the General your secrets, Vixen. You will get better, and then we will fight him together." When her eyes widened, he grinned. "I may have a few secrets of my own." When he felt Chase next to him, he looked up at the man. The one who claimed him as a son and part of his pack. "Alpha, she is like me." He knew Chase would know what he meant. She was a prisoner, made to torture and kill against her will. One who wanted out, but who was fighting against the bastard who held the control.

Chase sighed, placing a hand on his shoulder. "Then, we cannot let her die, son."

"Let me help," the pack doctor said, kneeling on the other side of Vixen. "That was one hell of a fight you put up there, lady," she said, placing a gentle hand on Vixen's shoulder. "My name's Doc Josie. I'm going to get you in the hospital and stitch some of these wounds up. You just need to promise not to try to kill me first. My mate doesn't like it when people try to do that."

A faint smile crossed Vixen's lips, and she whispered, "I don't think I could kill a bunny right now, Doc."

"I think we are going to put these on you first, just in case," a low voice said, as Ryker appeared, slapping a pair of silver cuffs on Vixen's wrists. When she cried out in pain, he shrugged. "Sorry, but my mate's right. It pisses me off when someone tries to hurt her."

Vixen glared at him, but she didn't argue. A low groan of pain left her as she was transferred to a stretcher, and then lifted to be carried to the hospital.

"I don't understand why you are helping me," she whispered, her eyes on the doctor. "I tried to capture one of your own."

"Sometimes, we are all required to do things we don't want to do. Things we have no control over. From what I just heard, you are trying to save people, Vixen, not kill them. You can't do that dead, now can you?"

"No." It was a whisper of uncertainty.

"Then, we need to fix you up so you can continue doing the good that you are doing." Jinx watched them walk away with Vixen before sighing. What the hell was he going to do now? "You, too, Jinx," Doc Josie said, looking back at him. When he didn't budge, she rested her hands lightly on her hips and narrowed her eyes on him. "I am not laying a hand on that woman until I look at your wounds first, Jinx Maddox, so I suggest you move your ass into my hospital room."

"You better go, son," Chase said gruffly. "The good doctor means what she says."

"Wait! Jinx! Wait!" Jinx turned to the voice and saw Raven come flying out of the front doors of the apartment complex next door. She ran to him, tears streaming down her cheeks as she slid her arms around his waist. "Thank you, Jinx. Thank you for everything. Jaxson told me that you were the reason they found me in the first place. And now," she paused, raising her wet eyes to his, "there is no doubt in my mind that you just saved my life. That woman was here to take me back to the General. I won't go back there. I won't!"

Ignoring the pain her arms around him caused, he awkwardly patted her back. "No, dragoness, you won't. I won't allow it."

"But you have orders to bring her back, too, don't you?" Rubi asked. "That's what Vixen said."

"He wants your sister. He won't stop sending people after her," Jinx told her quietly. "There is only one way to ensure she stays safe."

"You're going after him," she guessed, taking a step toward Jinx.

"There is no other way. I wanted to keep him alive because I'm trying to figure out who he answers to. He isn't the head of this monster, he is only a cog in the machine. But if I allow him to live, there is every chance Raven will die."

"What if he gets to you first, Son?" Steele asked. "Security around him will be tight now."

"Then I will go into the next life."

"Not acceptable," Angel snapped. "I refuse to hand you over to that bastard!"

"Maybe there's another way," Rubi said tentatively. "What if you use me?" A low growl began to fill the area, and she put a hand on her brother's arm. "No, Dax, hear me out. Raven and I look enough alike that I could pass for her. We're twins. I could go with Jinx, and maybe it will distract the General long enough for Jinx to take him out."

"That is the stupidest fucking idea I've ever heard of in my life," Dax yelled. "If you think for one second that I am going to let you sacrifice yourself for anyone like that, even our sister, Rubi Dreher, you better think again!"

"Raven has been through so much already, Dax. I don't want her to live her life in fear of that bastard coming after her. I am strong. I can handle it."

"No," Jinx cut in, effectively stalling the argument. "While what you are suggesting is very honorable, Rubi, you don't know what the General's like. How evil he is. You will not go anywhere near him." When she would have argued, he growled, "I can see into your mind, woman. I know what you are thinking, what you are planning if we don't agree. Do I need to have you handcuffed and your brother stand guard while I handle this?"

Her eyes widened in shock, and she slowly shook her head.

"Good."

"Jinx," Doc Josie interrupted, "I need to see to your wounds before your friend dies."

"She's not my friend," he muttered, pulling free of Raven's arms and following the doctor to the hospital. Normally, he would refuse treatment of any kind from anyone, but he decided to accept her help this time. He needed to get back to work. He had a General to hunt and eliminate.

18

Raven watched the powerful warrior walk to the hospital alone, her heart hurting for the man. He was strong, brave, courageous, but always alone. Not this time. "You need to go with him."

"What, baby?"

She turned to look at her mate. "When Jinx goes to take on the General, you need to go with him." Her gaze going to the rest of his team, she said, "All of you."

"Jinx works alone," Angel replied. "Trust me, I wish it weren't the way it was, but it is."

"Not this time." Raven grasped her mate's arm, looking at him imploringly. "Jinx saved my life just now, Jaxson. I would never have survived going back to the General. You know that woman is good. Really good. She was coming for me, and if he hadn't been here and fought her for me, that's where I would be. On my way back to that bastard with Vixen. We both know it. You need to go with him. After everything he's done, he deserves it."

Jaxson bowed his head, sighing. "It isn't that I don't agree with you, Raven. I do, but the man walks alone."

"Well, maybe it's time that changed."

JAXSON STOOD OUTSIDE THE HOSPITAL, indecision weighing on him. He knew Raven was right, and he wanted to help Jinx, but his reason for living was going to be at the White River Wolves compound without his protection until he returned. That pissed him off.

"You know it's the right thing to do," Raven said quietly, huddled up next to him, her arm around his waist, head on his chest.

"I do," he agreed. "I just don't like the thought of leaving you alone."

"She won't be alone, wolf." Jaxson glanced over his shoulder to see Dax, along with Rubi, RARE, and Chase with his White River Wolves team standing behind them. It was an impressive sight. "She will be with Rubi at all times."

"My wolves will also watch over Raven," Chase promised, his eyes glacier hard. "No one will get to her."

"As will the members of RARE, who will be staying behind," Angel said, standing proudly beside her mate.

"Dax stays, too," Jaxson demanded. When the dragon would have argued, Jaxson said, "I need my head in the game at all times. I can only do that knowing my mate is safe here. While I trust my team and pack to do what they can for her, you are her brother. You won't let anyone near her."

Dax nodded slowly, stepping close to clap a hand on his shoulder. "I promise you, she will be safe, brother."

"Sable, Trigger, and River, you will stay behind, too," Chase ordered. "Slade will take you off all other enforcer duties until we return. Your main priority is Raven."

Jaxson's jaw clenched, and he gave his alpha a nod of gratitude. "Thank you."

"What's going on?"

Jaxson turned to the man who stood at the top of the hospital steps, a man who would never ask for help from anyone. One with the weight of the world on his shoulders. Now, he was going to see what having a pack meant.

"We're coming with you, Jinx," Jaxson told him. "You are not alone in this." When Jinx shook his head, Jaxson grinned. "I'm afraid you don't have a choice, man. After everything you have done for my mate, I'm not staying behind."

"And for my mate," Xavier said, stepping forward. "You took out the man who haunted Janie's dreams. You made her feel safe again. I'm coming with you."

"There is no debt to pay," Jinx said, his hands clenched tightly into fists at his sides.

"We will fight by your side," Aiden said, moving beside his brother. "As pack and as friends."

"Sapphire and I go with you, nephew," Bane said, crossing his arms over his chest, his tone broking no argument. "You are family." He stopped there, as if that said it all... which it did.

When Jinx looked as if he were going to protest again, Steele smiled. "It's a useless argument, my son. We are coming."

"Agreed," Chase growled. "You spend your life

protecting others, Jinx. A lone wolf in the midst of hell. It is time you see that you are not truly alone."

"I am the General's assassin," Jinx muttered, his eyes going from their natural deep brown color to a dark green, giving away the deep emotion he felt. "I take lives."

"You are family," Chase stated, climbing the stairs to stand beside him. "You are pack, and we will remind you of that every damn day if we need to, Son. You are ours."

Jaxson watched as Jinx struggled against his emotions and wondered what it must have been like to grow up without the love of his parents. He may have lost his entire family and pack years ago, but they were the ones who had molded him into the man he was today. Without them, who knew where he would have ended up. This man in front of them had been raised by the devil himself, but had overcome all obstacles. He was a fierce warrior who fought for what he believed in. Yes, he was the General's assassin, but he did not take innocent lives. He was honorable and worthy.

Letting go of Raven, Jaxson stepped forward. "You kill those who are evil, Jinx. You save the innocent. You are no different than any of us here. We've all done things we aren't proud of. Things we had no choice over. In that, we are the same. We go with you, my friend. I owe you a debt I can never repay, but I start trying today."

"There is no debt," Jinx said quietly, a muscle in his jaw ticking. "It's what pack does."

Jaxson grinned, scaling the stairs to clasp the man's hand. "You got that right. Now, let's go kick some General ass."

19

Hidden behind a large cropping of rock, Jaxson watched Jinx pull up in front of the large building on a dark blue Harley that looked brand new. They were deep in the middle of a forest in California, but somehow, Jinx had managed to get that damn motorcycle there. The guy was an enigma, hard and mysterious, and Jaxson was glad he was on their side.

"Nice," Xavier breathed into the comms. "I need to get me one of those."

"Your mate would kick your ass," his brother responded. "Then she'd come after me."

Xavier chuckled. "It might be worth it just to see that."

"I'd pay to see it," Charlotte chimed in.

"I got a twenty to throw in the pot," Sapphire said, her voice a mere whisper.

Jaxson swore he saw Jinx's lips twitch at the conversation, but then his face was that blank, unyielding mask again he always wore. Jinx had refused the ear comms, but Jaxson knew he didn't need them. They were too far away for the wolf to actually hear them, but he had abilities beyond any of the members of RARE. There was no doubt in Jaxson's mind that Jinx knew everything that was going on around him.

"I think my buddy Jinx just put in a fifty," Jaxson muttered, chuckling when Jinx gave a small nod. "Yep, he did."

"You all suck," Aiden growled playfully.

Jinx knocked on the door, then disappeared inside the building when it opened for him. Jaxson held his breath until he heard him say, "Where's the General?" While he'd refused the ear comm, he had allowed Jaxson to tag him with a listening device so the team would be able to hear him, even if they couldn't see him.

What Jaxson heard next shocked the hell out of him. "In his quarters with Ebony." It was Jeremiah's voice. The fucking bear was there. After months of trying to find him, he finally turned up when they least expected it.

"Jeremiah," Angel whispered. "Thank fuck."

"You may want to leave, bear," they heard Jinx warn him quietly.

"I'm not going anywhere," was the growled response.

There was silence, and then, "Make sure these doors are open in ten minutes."

"Done."

"I'm going to kick that bear's ass," Angel muttered through the comms.

Jaxson kept his gaze on the door Jinx had gone through, listening intently. He hated sending the man in alone, even if he did work for the General. It wasn't like he had a choice, and this time, he was going in empty-handed. Everyone there with him knew that meant Jinx's life was on the line.

There was a knock, and then, "Jinx, so nice of you to join us."

Ebony. The bitch made his skin crawl. Jaxson held back a growl as he heard, "Touch me again and I'll cut your fucking hand off."

A small grin appeared, and Jaxson muttered, "That's our boy."

"Jinx. I sent you after something of mine. Where is it?"

Jaxson bared his fangs, unable to stop the growl that started deep in his chest this time. The bastard acted as if Raven was his fucking property. His woman belonged to no one except him; as he belonged to her. The General would die for that comment alone.

"I wasn't the only one you sent, was I?" Jinx's voice was low, deadly. "You know I work alone."

"Where is Vixen?" Ebony asked, and Jaxson got the impression she had moved further away from Jinx. "She hasn't checked in yet."

"She failed," Jinx growled. "As will anyone else you send."

"Is that a threat?' the General snapped.

"I don't make threats," Jinx countered. "The woman is off limits. Touch her, and you answer to me."

"Answer to you?" the General sneered. "I think it's time you learn who's boss, you little shit."

"That's our cue," Angel said, and Jaxson heard the whisper of movement as the team began to make their way to the building. His gun in hand, he slipped from behind the rocks.

"First guard down," Sapphire murmured.

Jaxson was flying through the trees near the building when he heard Trace mutter, "Second and third gone."

"Fourth one eliminated," Charlotte said in a cold, hard tone.

Jaxson hit the door, yanking it open to see Jeremiah waiting on the other side. "Move," he snarled, shoving past him. "That bastard is mine."

He didn't hear what the bear said, and he didn't really care. His main objective was to get to the son of a bitch who had held his mate for a year, torturing her. The fucker was going to die.

"We will deal with you later, Jeremiah," he heard Angel snap. "Right now, we have a General to take down."

"There's more at stake here than the General," Jeremiah warned. "You need to call your team off, Angel."

"No fucking way!" Jaxson growled, not slowing down. He could smell the bastard. He was close.

"You dare defy me? I was right, wasn't I?" The General's voice came to him, driving his wolf into a frenzy.

"About some things," Jinx acknowledged.

"But wrong about so many others," Ebony said before there was a loud bang. Then another. "The bitch he wanted so badly is free, Jinx," Jaxson heard. "I will let her go. I don't give a shit about her, but you are mine. You work for me. Don't forget that, or everyone you care for will die. And I do mean everyone."

Jaxson shifted mid-run, quickly sliding out of his clothes and leaving them behind, as he sprinted the rest of the way down the hall. A loud howl ripped from his throat when he saw the General leaning up against a desk, his hands covering his chest where two dark red splotches of blood were blooming out from bullet wounds. Jaxson didn't care.

The man wasn't dead yet, but he was going to be. Springing from the doorway, he hit the General full in the chest with his large front paws, locking his powerful jaws around his throat. With a loud roar, he bit down hard and yanked, tearing the evil bastard's throat out. It was over before it even started. The General's lifeless body crumpled to the floor in a pool of his own blood. Jaxson snarled loudly, standing over him before throwing his head back and howling loudly over and over again in victory. He was dead. The fucker who haunted all of their nightmares was finally dead, and Jaxson had served justice for his mate. He wasn't stupid enough to think the hell they all lived in was over. But this part of it was.

He turned toward his team as they entered the room after they finished sweeping the rest of the building and howled again, baring his teeth. Angel stopped just inside, looking around, her jaw clenched tightly. "Where's Jinx?" Jaxson froze, his gaze following Angel's. "Where's my son?"

"He went with Ebony," Jeremiah said, his large presence filling the room behind the others. "Slipped out through a hidden panel in the connecting room. She didn't give him a choice."

"I heard," Angel whispered, shaking her head as her eyes misted over with tears. "I was just hoping I was wrong."

Jaxson let out one more loud howl, this one more of misery as he realized his friend, the one reason he'd managed to get close to the man who had hurt his mate, was gone. Shifting, his chest heaving as he struggled to catch his breath, he snarled, "We'll get him back, Angel. He's family. He's coming home."

"Not right now," Jeremiah said quietly. "You need to understand that everything has changed. Yes, you took out the General, but you just put into effect something I have been trying to prevent for months. Something even worse than the General's reign of terror."

"What the hell are you talking about, Jeremiah?" Angel demanded, glaring at him. "We've been looking for you, you asshole! You've been avoiding us!"

Angel was mad as hell, but it didn't seem to affect the bear. He nodded, glancing down at where the General lay at his feet. "Yes, I have." Sighing, he raked a hand through his hair and shook his head. "Do you really think I want to be away from my mate like this? She's my fucking world. But with the General gone, you've just placed someone even worse in charge."

"Who?" Angel demanded.

Jaxson silently accepted a pair of jogging pants from Nico, slipping them on as he watched the exchange. Had he fucked up? "Ebony shot the General," he said, bringing the bear's attention to him. "There's a good chance he would have died anyway."

"Ebony has been pulling the General's strings for a long time," Jeremiah told them. "She's the one who really decides who comes and goes, who lives or dies. And now, she's just moved up into his place, somewhere she's always wanted to be, but hadn't yet had the opportunity to snatch for herself. If you think the General was bad, she's ten times worse."

"Fuck," Nico growled, slamming his fist into the wall next to him. "We are fighting an uphill battle, aren't we?"

"Always," Jeremiah said, turning away.

"Jeremiah, you need to come back with us," Angel said, stepping toward him. "Rikki needs you."

Jeremiah hung his head, then rasped, "I can't, Angel. There is more at stake here than Rikki and I."

"She's in the hospital, Jeremiah. The General's men almost killed her. She's been in a coma for months."

A loud roar ripped from the bear's throat, and his claws shot through his fingertips.

"She won't wake up. She needs you."

"Is she...is she in pain?" Jeremiah demanded, his powerful shoulders shaking.

"No, not right now," Angel admitted. "The doctor says she is in a healing sleep." When Jeremiah didn't respond, Angel took a step closer. "Jeremiah, I think if you were there, she would wake up. Please, come home."

"Stop!" he ordered, holding up his hand, not looking at them. "I can't come back. Not yet. That's final. Please, take care of my mate until I can."

Jaxson watched the man walk away from them, his shoulders slumped, the scent of his pain nearly suffocating them.

"He loves her so much," Storm said, her eyes wide in wonder. "I don't understand why he won't go home to her."

"He is staying for the same reason my son does," Steele told her, reaching over to lace his fingers through hers. "As much as he loves Rikki, she's safe right now, while so many others aren't. They are trying to stop an all-out war."

Angel nodded, sliding her Glock back into its holster as she went to leave the room, motioning them to follow. "Yes, and they need our help. So, instead of standing around talking, let's get our asses home and start planning."

"I think we may have another problem, Angel."

Angel glanced back at Bane raising an eyebrow. "What?"

Inhaling deeply, he said, "I am assuming the scents in the room that I don't know are the General's and Ebony's, correct? There are no others?"

"Yes," she said, her eyes narrowing in confusion. "What's going on, Bane?'

"When we rescued Raven, I picked up two scents there."

"Ebony and Amber."

"One was my mate."

"Fuck," Jaxson drawled, his eyes widening as understanding dawned. "Please, tell me that bitch Ebony is not your mate."

Bane slowly shook his head, his dark eyes clouding with pain. "No, she's not, which means Amber is."

"Oh no!" Sapphire gasped through the comms. "She's the one that's missing."

"Fuck," Jaxson growled, his heart going out to the man. "We'll find her, Bane."

Bane didn't reply. He just left the room, walking down the hall ahead of them.

"I refuse to lose anyone else to that son of a bitch or his daughter," Jaxson snarled. "We will find her, Bane. I promise you that."

Bane paused, his shoulders stiffening, and then he looked back. His eyes were a swirling mixture of dark brown and yellow, his fangs bared, as he growled, "Yes, we will."

20

Raven sat on the edge of the bed, her head bowed, her arms wrapped tightly around one of Jaxson's pillows. Inhaling deeply, she breathed his scent, letting it flow through her body. Tears filled her eyes, slowly sliding down her cheeks. She knew he was safe, knew he was on his way home to her, but she'd been so terrified that she had sent him to his death. Her mind was going crazy with different scenarios that could have happened, even though she knew what had taken place, but she couldn't seem to stop it. She needed him home. Needed him to hold her and tell her everything was going to be okay.

Inhaling deeply again, a soft sob slipped out. She shoved her face into the pillow, hoping no one in the other room would hear her. Even with the threat from the General eliminated, they had all refused to leave until Jaxson came home to her.

"Raven?" She heard her sister's voice, but just buried her head deeper into the pillow, feeling so weak and powerless. What had happened to her? How had she become so spineless? "It's going to be all right, Sis," Rubi promised, sitting down next to her. "Jaxson's plane landed a while ago. He will be here soon." Raven felt an arm slip around her, and then Rubi leaned her head on her shoulder. "I've missed you so much, Raven. I am so sorry."

"I've missed you, too," she mumbled into the pillow.

"I hate them so much for what they did to you," Rubi whispered. "Sometimes, at night, I think about our parents' part in everything, and I want them to suffer like you did. Worse than you did."

Raven slowly raised her head and leaned it against the top of her sister's.

"Does that make me a horrible person?" Rubi asked, swiping at the tears that ran down her cheeks.

"If it does, then it makes me one, too," Raven confessed quietly. "I've felt that way since the very beginning."

"You knew what our parents did?"

"Yes," Raven replied, staring into the darkness of the bedroom. "Perez used to gloat about it. He thought it was funny that he could get someone to sell off their own child."

"Oh, Raven." She heard the sorrow in her sister's voice and realized Rubi had suffered just as much as she had, only in a different way. "I wish it would have been me," Rubi cried. "Every night I asked myself why they took you and not me. I would have gladly gone through all of it for you, Raven."

And she would have. Raven didn't need to scent the truth to know how Rubi felt. The bond they had was strong, stronger than most siblings. Not only that, but she'd heard what Rubi said the other day, offering herself to the General in Raven's place. "I have no idea why things turned out the way they did, Rubi, but I'm glad I was the one who was taken and not you."

"You are?" Rubi sniffled. "Why?"

"Two reasons. First of all, I love you so much, and the thought of you out there somewhere, alone and defenseless, would have killed me."

"It almost did me," Rubi admitted. "I started training harder. I went to the warrior grounds every single day, and they let me. They helped me hone my skills and promised to help me rescue you if I ever found you, but none of them would believe me when I told them Dad and Mom sold you. That's when I found out they had already talked to Dad, and he had them convinced that I was going insane because you were missing. Which meant they were just catering to me." Rubi shrugged. "I didn't care at that point. They were still training me, and that was all that mattered. Even if they didn't help me when I found you, I was going to be able to rescue you myself."

"You would have, too," Raven said, sitting the pillow aside and reaching over to capture Rubi's hand in her own. "I have no doubt you would have saved me."

"What was your other reason?"

"What?"

"You said there were two reasons you were glad it was you who was taken and not me?"

Raven laughed, squeezing her sister's hand gently. "Fate has a funny way of working things out sometimes."

"Yeah?"

"I met Jaxson," Raven whispered, a slow smile spreading across her lips. "That might not have happened if I wasn't taken by Perez's men. I went through hell for over a year, first with Perez, and then the General, but I would do it all again for that man. He's my world."

"As you are mine, sweet mate."

Raven's heart jumped at Jaxson's words, her lips parting in a surprised gasp as she sprang from the bed. "You're home!"

Rubi laughed, rising and giving Raven a quick hug. "I love you, Raven," she said, running a hand gently down Raven's hair. "I'll see you tomorrow."

"Love you, too," Raven said, her gaze never leaving Jaxson's. He was home. Safe.

The minute Rubi was out of the room, the door clicking shut quietly behind her, Raven closed the distance between them and wrapped her arms around his neck, clinging to him tightly. "I was so worried."

"I'm right here, baby. Nothing to worry about."

Tugging on his hand, she guided him over to the bed. "Sit."

A low growl slid up his throat at her order, but he did as she said.

Kneeling in front of him, Raven began to untie his shoelaces. "Tell me what happened." She'd been given a quick rundown, but wanted details.

She listened carefully to his story as she slipped his shoes off, his socks following, pausing to interrupt him when he was only partway through. "I don't understand. Who's Jeremiah?"

Standing, Raven grasped his tee shirt and slid it up over his head, her eyes going hungrily to his bare skin.

"He's Rikki's mate."

"Rikki?" Her brow furrowed as she tried to remember where she'd heard that name. She gasped when it came to her. "Your teammate who's in the hospital? Jade told me about her. Is she going to be okay? And what is Jeremiah doing with the General if he's Rikki's mate?"

Unable to resist, Raven reached out and traced her fingers from his collarbone down the middle of his chest to his abdominal muscles. A low groan slipped from Jaxson's lips, and he caught her hand in his. "You want the story or me, mate? You can't have both right now. I don't have the control."

That was an easy question to answer. "You."

Her eyes widened when she saw his gaze go wolf, and then his claws were slicing through the front of her shirt. She stood still as he went for her pants next, ridding her of her bra and underwear just as quickly. She stood naked before him in mere seconds, breathing heavily as her body strummed with excitement.

"You have too many clothes on," she panted, her mouth watering as she watched his hands go to the snap of his jeans. "Mine!" she snarled, swatting his hands away and letting her own claws come out to play.

"Shit! Raven!"

A slow, sensual smile crossed her face as she ran the tip of one claw over his chest, slowly circling his beaded nipple before going to the other one. Leaning over, she licked at his nipple, biting down gently.

"Raven!" He hollered her name as his body jumped. "Baby, please."

Ignoring him, she took her time, licking her way slowly down his treasure trail, sucking and nibbling along the way. Running the back of her claw over his fully erect cock, she growled in satisfaction as he arched into her. Sliding one of the sharp claws under the waistband on the side of his jeans, she ripped them open, easily tearing the cloth apart. Soon, she had the denim stripped away, but instead of taking him into her mouth the way she wanted to, she crawled up his body, her knees on the bed as she straddled his hips. "I want you inside me."

"Hell yeah!"

When he would have grabbed her hips, she growled in warning, showing her fangs, wanting him to know she was in charge.

"Ah, shit, Raven. You don't know how much that turns me on."

She reached down and grasped his cock, and then slowly guided it to where she wanted him. At first, she just let the hard, velvety tip inside of her, then she slowly began to lower herself down on him.

"Raven," he groaned, bucking his hips up into her. "You're so tight, baby. So hot, wet."

She let him move at first, then tightened her thighs, holding his hips still. His eyes darkened, and he threw his head back, his mouth open, his fangs long and large as he tried to push deeper into her. She wanted to feel them sink in her skin. Needed him to claim her again. But first, she was going to claim him.

Raven began to move, slowly at first, loving the growls and groans coming from her mate. He brought his hands up to rest them on her hips, but didn't try to take over when she growled in warning. She wanted to be in charge. Needed to be.

"Raven. Move, dammit!"

Her eyes glued to where she'd left her mate bite on Jaxson's shoulder, then ground down on his hard erection, beginning to move faster and faster. She felt her beast come closer to the surface and watched as a layer of fire flowed over her body, matching the one burning inside of her. "Won't hurt you," she gasped, as it slid over her skin to his.

"I know," he rasped around his fangs. "Didn't hurt last time."

"Our fire never hurts our mates."

Jaxson tightened his hold on Raven's hips and thrust deep, his body shuddering. "I'm so close, Raven!"

So was she. Knowing she wasn't going to last much longer, Raven opened her mouth, lowered her head, and sank her teeth deep into Jaxson's skin, loving the way he shouted as he began to pulse deep inside her. Finding his own mate mark, he bit down, and she splintered apart on top of him.

"So, Jeremiah refused to come back?"

"Yeah," Jaxson growled, anger filling him at the thought of Jeremiah leaving his mate alone. "Angel says it's because he is trying to stop a war, but I don't understand, Raven. If you were in trouble, there isn't anything out there that could keep me from you."

"That's just it, my love," she whispered, tracing her fingers over his temple, and then moving down to cup his jaw in her hand. "Rikki isn't in trouble right now. You said yourself the doctor said she seems to be in a healing sleep."

"Yes, but…"

"Jaxson, Rikki is safe. She's here, with us, and Jeremiah knows we are her family. We will take care of her while he is out there doing everything he can to prevent any more harm from coming her way."

Jaxson nodded, even though he was still pissed. "Yeah, we will."

"From what you've said, it sounds like he loves Rikki very much."

"He does."

"Then, all we can do is respect his wishes and watch over his mate that he has trusted in our care."

Sighing, Jaxson held Raven close. "How did you get to be so smart?"

Raven giggled, kissing him on the cheek. "Don't tell my brother, but he might have had a hand in it."

Jaxson threw his head back and laughed. "No way in hell will I tell that arrogant dragon anything you just said. He's hard enough to live with now as it is."

"Isn't he wonderful?" Raven whispered, snuggling close.

"Yes, he is, baby."

"Jaxson?"

"Yeah?"

"Do you think Amber is alive?" He heard the catch in his mate's voice, and it tore him up knowing how much his answer meant to her right now. Unfortunately, he would always be honest with her, and he couldn't give her the one he knew she wanted to hear.

"I don't know, Raven. Ebony has her locked up tight somewhere, and no matter how hard we try, we haven't been able to find her."

"That's what you've been doing when you go to your meetings with the team," Raven realized.

"Yes," he said. "I didn't tell you because I didn't want to get your hopes up."

"You haven't found anything at all?"

"No, we haven't, but we won't stop trying."

"Thank you," she whispered quietly, tracing a circle pattern on his chest. "She's done so much for me, Jaxson. She's my best friend, like a sister to me. I can't stand the thought of her going through the things I did."

Lowering his head, he closed his eyes and inhaled her scent deeply. "You know what you mean to me, Raven?"

"Yes," came the quiet response.

"Well, Amber means the same to Bane."

Raven froze, then raised her head slowly to look at him. "Bane's her mate?"

"Yeah. He scented both Ebony and Amber when we rescued you in D.C., and knew one of them was his, he just didn't know which one. He figured it out on this last trip to California."

"Thank God it's not Ebony," Raven said with a shudder.

Jaxson silently agreed, but wondered if it was any better that it was Amber. They had no idea if the girl was dead or alive, and heaven help them all if she had already gone on into the next world. Bane was a quiet man, one who seemed to hold everything inside. A dangerous man with a shitload of power locked down tight. Once he let it loose, Jaxson had an idea that everything in his path would be destroyed.

21

Chase stared at the woman in the chair across from him, letting her feel the full force of his alpha power. He saw her stiffen, but she didn't move. Part of that was probably because she was in handcuffs and bound to the chair she was sitting in, with a chain through each cuff and wrapped around the metal legs of the chair. He would guess a lot of it had to do with her training, though. She was an assassin, who had been taught to bide her time, wait for an opening, and then strike. He was about to give her that opening and see if she took it. Several people had advised him against it, but he trusted Jinx, and Jinx seemed to think there was good in Vixen. They were about to find out.

"Your name?"

Cocking an eyebrow, she stayed silent.

"You can cooperate, or I can throw you in a cell for a while. Up to you."

For the past two weeks, she'd been chained to a hospital bed. When Doc Josie finally informed him that it

was okay to move her, he had sent Sable, Silver, and Charlotte to get her with orders that she be dressed in the
clothes she'd shown up in and then brought to the room
they were in now. One he used for questioning. He had
sent Dax, Steele, and Storm as backup. She hadn't given
them any trouble… yet.

She was quiet for a moment, then seemed to come to a
decision. "Vixen."

"I know what the General calls you. I want to know
your real name."

Her eyes seemed to cloud over, and her jaw tightened
as she replied, "That is my real name." When he stared at
her in silence, an eyebrow raised, she shrugged. "I've been
with the General since I was three years old. I don't
remember my life before him."

"Yes, you do," he said, when he saw a flicker of something in her gaze. "Tell me what you remember."

She shrugged, her eyes never leaving his. "I remember
cold. Hunger. Fear."

"Was that before or after the General found you?"

"Both."

"How long have you been with the General?"

"Long enough."

He couldn't refute that.

Chase nodded, leaning forward to place his forearms
on the table. "Look, Vixen, I'm going to be straight with
you because my son seems to think you are worth it."

"Your son?" He saw the confusion in her eyes before it
was quickly masked.

"Jinx."

Her eyes went to Steele. "I thought Jinx was his son?"

"I am Jinx's biological father," Steele told her. "Chase is mated to Jinx's mother, Angel."

Vixen's gaze went to where Angel stood behind Chase, following his lead this time. "Am I the only one who finds this odd?"

"The General is dead, Vixen."

He saw the shock when what he said hit her, but she recovered quickly. "Bullshit."

"He is," Angel said, stepping forward. "Shot by Ebony twice, and then one of my wolves tore his throat out."

Vixen seemed to be weighing Angel's words, and then she asked, "What about Ebony?"

"Sounds like she's taking over for her father."

"Shit."

"Our sentiments exactly," Chase said, tapping his fingers on the table. "Vixen, you are free to go," he said, motioning to Dax.

"What?"

"As far as we know, Ebony thinks you are dead," Angel told her. "Jinx told the General you failed in your mission, which to them would have meant death. We know you are in a position you have no desire to be in, just as my son is, and we are letting you go. I would suggest you hide yourself, though, unless you want to end up on Ebony's hit list."

"I hide from no one."

"Then, there is every chance you will die."

The door to the room opened and Silver walked in, Vixen's weapons in her hands. Setting them on the table, she moved back to stand next to Steele and Storm.

Vixen stood once the chains were removed, her gaze moving slowly around the room. "I don't understand," she confessed. "You know who I am, the things I've done. Why would you let me go?"

"Because Jinx asked it of me," Chase said, taking a step away from her so she didn't feel caged in. Dax moved back over to his corner, leaving the path to the door wide open.

Vixen seemed to hesitate, and then she reached for her weapons slowly. "Where's Jinx?" she asked, as she slid one sai into her boot.

"With Ebony," Angel said through gritted teeth. "She gave him an ultimatum."

"He works for her or she kills the ones he cares about?" Vixen guessed, sliding the other sai into her other boot.

"Yes."

"I've always hated that bitch."

"She's going to kill my son, isn't she?" Angel whispered, reaching out to grasp Chase's arm. He drew her close, knowing she needed his touch right now.

Vixen stared at them for a long moment, then slowly shook her head. "No, she won't kill him. She needs him for now."

"For now." Angel latched onto those words, and Chase felt the pain slam through her.

"For now is enough," Vixen said, strapping a gun to her hip. "It will keep him alive until we can get him out of there."

"We?"

Vixen raised her head, her gaze clashing with his. "I don't run, Alpha. I fight. Now that I'm not tied to that son of a bitch, it means I can fight against all that he stood for out in the open. I need to make sure the children are safe, but I will be back soon."

"How soon?" Angel demanded, her hand tightening on Chase's arm.

"As soon as I can," Vixen promised, slipping the rest of her knives into various spots on her leather pants. With one last look at them, she turned and walked from the room.

"She's coming back," Angel said, her nails digging into Chase's skin. "She's going to help us."

"Yes." Chase had heard the truth in the woman's words and scented no lie. She would be back, but this time, she would be on their side.

22

Raven stood in front of the large cottage-style house she'd grown up in, now painted a light green with white trim and large brick around the bottom. She had been happy there, with her sister and brother, and although she wasn't particularly close with her parents, she'd loved them.

"You don't have to do this, Raven."

Dax's voice was a low growl, and she knew he was angry at her decision to face the people who had ruined her life. If he'd had his way, she and Rubi would never be within five states of them again. But she was having a hard time moving on, and she was beginning to suspect she had a really good reason to do that now. One she still needed to tell Jaxson about. Her hand slowly came up to rest on her stomach and she leaned into her mate. "Yes, I do."

"I hate them," Rubi snapped, slamming the car door and walking over to stand by her. "I don't understand how they can get away with what they did."

"They won't," Dax promised. Raven glanced back to see her brother's arm encircle Sable's waist, pulling her near. Her gaze went to where Silver and Charlotte were exiting Sable's vehicle. And then to another SUV that had just pulled to a stop near theirs. Angel emerged, Chase at her side. Then came Trace and Jade, along with Nico and Sapphire.

"You all didn't have to come," she whispered, still in shock that they had.

"Of course, we did," Angel said, smiling gently at her. "You are one of us now, Raven, and we love you. We will always be here for you."

Raven's eyes filled with tears, and she moved closer to Jaxson. She was so glad she wasn't alone anymore. Not only did she have her brother and sister again, but she had more family than she'd ever dreamed of. "Thank you."

"What the hell is going on out here?" Raven caught her breath, a small shudder running through her. She'd know that voice anywhere. Straightening her spine, she turned to look at the man who now stood in front of them. Tall, stocky, and in a rage.

"Hello, Father."

He stiffened, his eyes widening when they saw her, and then he cursed loudly. "What are you doing here, Raven? Dammit! You've just sentenced our entire family to death."

Raven felt the low growl deep in Jaxson's chest before she actually heard it. "You will watch how you speak to my mate," he snarled.

"Who the hell do you think you are?"

"Oh, the Fates! Raven?" Her mother flew out of the house running toward her, but then seemed to catch herself. Her gaze went to her husband, and then back to Raven. "Oh no! How are you here? You can't be here, Raven! He will kill us all!"

"You are more worried about your own death than that of your child?" Chase growled, coming to stand right behind her.

"I'm worried about all of my family," her mother argued.

"You sold your daughter to save yourselves," Chase growled. "Is that correct?"

"Well," her mother looked over at her, her eyes wide and scared. "We didn't have a choice!"

"There is always a choice, Mother," Rubi said, walking over to Raven and linking their arms together. "You chose wrong."

"Dammit, who are all of these people?" her father demanded.

Raven's bottom lip trembled, and then she took a deep breath. That, she could answer. "They are the people who care about me. The ones who saved me from the hell you threw me into. They put their own lives on the line for me, because to them, I am worth it. *They* are my family."

"They are *our* family," Dax said, walking over to stand beside Jaxson, his mate's hand in his.

"Dax…"

"No," he cut in, his voice hard and unyielding. "You sold our sister to someone, who in turn sold her to one of the meanest, most vile men out there. She was starved, sliced into, tortured."

"She looks fine now," her father stated, as if what she'd gone through that past year meant nothing to him, and she could tell that it didn't. As long as he was all right, he didn't seem to care what had happened to her. "She needs to go back. If he comes looking for her…"

"No!" a voice thundered, and Raven gasped when she saw the man who appeared, stalking around the corner of her parents' house.

She dropped to her knees, head to the ground, Rubi quickly doing the same beside her. Her body trembled at the rage in the air, and she fought to catch her breath. Sweat beaded up on her forehead and she fought the urge to cry.

"Raven, what's going on?" Jaxson asked, trying to tug her back to her feet.

"Jaxson, get down here," she hissed. "Please, hurry."

He knelt beside her, but refused to touch his head to the ground. Instead, he stared in confusion at what was taking place before him.

"Jaxson, please."

"He is fine, little dragoness."

The deep, rich tenor had her entire body shaking as she whispered, "I apologize for my mate, King Bartholomew. He does not know our ways."

She felt her king stop in front of her, and then he reached down and gently took her arm in his large hand. "Rise, little one. Stand so that I can see you."

Raven struggled to her feet with Jaxson's help, and said shakily, "Thank you, your highness." Slowly, she let herself raise her head and look at the man. She'd never actually met him in person before, but everyone knew what the king looked like, and there was no mistaking the fact that he was royalty by the way he was dressed. The king was huge, with long blond hair flowing down his back and snapping dark eyes that were lit with anger. Dark green and blue robes lined with gold covered him, chains of gold around his neck and gold rings on his fingers.

"Daxton Dreher," he said, inclining his head toward her brother where he was rising to his feet. "I've heard there has been a disturbance connected with your family. I sent soldiers to check several times, but they could find nothing, so I've been having the house monitored. Care to tell me what this is all about?"

"I am the head of this household," Raven's father said, taking a step toward the king, stopping abruptly when two of the king's guards stepped forward. "Everything should go through me," he protested.

"Are you questioning me?" the king growled, turning to look at her father, baring impressive fangs.

It looked as if her father would argue, but then he slowly shook his head. "No, your excellency."

When the king turned back to Dax and raised an eyebrow, Dax stepped forward, bowing his head in acknowledgment before saying, "When I came home after serving you, my king, I found out my parents had sold my sister, Raven, after being threatened with death. My other sister, Rubi, and I managed to track her to a Colombian drug lord, Philip Perez, where we found out she was then sold to the General."

"The General?"

"It's a long story."

"One I need to hear?"

"Not the whole thing, unless you would like to. Right now, what you need to know is that for the past year Raven has been through hell."

"Raven?" the king said, turning kind eyes toward her. "Are you okay now, child? Are you safe?"

Raven nodded, moving closer to Jaxson, slipping an arm around his waist. "Yes, your highness. The General was trying to figure out what kind of shifter I was, but I didn't break. No matter what they did, I didn't tell them, and I never shifted."

"Are you sure?"

"Yes," she promised. "I made a promise to myself that I would protect our kind, and you. I didn't break."

A gentle smile crossed the king's lips, and he reached out to place a hand on her head. "Very good, my child. And this is your mate?"

"Yes. Jaxson."

"And they are?" he asked, sweeping his arm out in a wide gesture to all of the people surrounding them.

"They are my family," she said, a tremulous smile crossing her face. "They came for me, King. Saved me." Turning, she motioned toward Chase and Angel. "Chase Montgomery is the alpha of the White River Wolves in Colorado, and Angel is his mate. They have accepted my brother and sister as part of their pack, and me, too."

"And that is what you want?"

"Yes," she said, smiling again. "They've made me whole again, sir. Happy."

"And you, Daxton?" his eyes going to where Dax held tightly to Sable's hand. "You have found your mate among the wolves, as well?"

"Yes, my king."

The king nodded, his gaze sweeping the area again, before landing on Chase. "Chase Montgomery, take care of my dragons."

"You have my word," Chase vowed, bowing his head to the king.

Running his hand gently down her head, the king turned to smile at Rubi. "I've been watching you practice, Rubi Dreher. You are a fierce warrior. If I could, I would call you to serve as part of my guard."

"Maybe you should anyway," Rubi shot back, making him throw his head back and laugh.

Then, he turned to Raven's parents. "Grady and Dora Dreher, you will come with us for sentencing."

A soft gasp left Raven's lips as she realized her parents were going to stand trial for what they did to her.

"Sentencing?" Jaxson asked softly.

"They will have to stand before a jury of five," Raven explained quietly. "They will decide my parents' fate."

"For what?" her father snarled, struggling against the guard who slapped a large, thick gold cuff on his wrist.

"How about for fucking with one of my dragons?" the king roared, his blond hair flying out behind him as the wind kicked up around them. "You will stand trial, and you better pray to the Gods above that they are more merciful than I would be. Because I just want to snap your neck right now, you poor excuse of a dragon!"

"No! Please, have mercy!" her mother wailed, clinging to her mate. "We just did what we thought was best."

"You thought it was best to sell your child?" the king said incredulously. "What you should have done was come to me. Instead, you sentenced your child to a year in hell. You will receive more than that."

Gold cuffs were slapped on her mother's wrists, the king nodded in their direction, and then they were around the back of the house and gone. As if they'd never been there.

"Did that just happen?" Sable breathed. "Did we really just meet the king of the freaking dragons?"

"Did you see how fast he put the smack down?" Silver whispered. "That is one man you do not want to mess with."

Raven listened to her friends talk, but she couldn't take her eyes from where her parents had just disappeared. "They're gone."

Jaxson bent to kiss her gently on the lips, and asked, "You okay, sweet mate?"

"I don't know," she answered truthfully. Turning into his arms, she slipped her arms around his neck and leaned into him. "But I know I will be."

Raven's heart filled with pure joy as she smiled at the woman across from her. "You're sure?"

Doc Josie nodded, her eyes alight with excitement. "I'm positive, Raven. I am so happy for you and Jaxson."

"He doesn't know, yet," Raven admitted. "I wanted to see you before I said anything."

The doctor placed a gentle hand on her arm and said, "I think he is going to be thrilled, as will the rest of the pack. We can all use a little happiness in our lives right now."

Raven covered Doc Josie's hand with hers. "I agree."

Saying her goodbyes, Raven left the doctor's office and walked down the hall, turning to the left and walking down another one. Stopping in the doorway of the room where Rikki lay, she hesitated before making her way to the bed. She stared at the beautiful woman for a moment, then reached out to slowly run a hand down her long, black hair. "Hey, Rikki," she whispered softly. "My name's Raven. I've heard so much about you from my mate,

Jaxson." She watched closely, but there was no reaction, not that she expected one. The woman lay motionless, except for the slight movement of her chest with each breath she took.

Moving a chair over near the bed, Raven sat down and slipped her hand in the other woman's, squeezing it gently. "I've been told that you are in a healing sleep right now, and that you could wake up at any time. I really hope that's true, Rikki, because you are very missed here." Rubbing a hand over Rikki's arm, knowing contact was important for a shifter, she went on, "I haven't been with the White River Wolves for very long. I actually just came here a few weeks ago, after RARE and Chase's team of wolves saved me from the General. I'd been his captive for the past year." Raven's eyes widened in shock when a small sound of distress left Rikki's lips and the hand in hers clenched and unclenched, before grasping her hand tightly. "It's okay, Rikki," she rushed to reassure the other woman who was moving around in agitation. "You're going to be okay."

Reaching over, Raven pushed the red alert button by the bed hoping to get one of the nurse's attention, pushing it again several times when there was no answer.

"Raven, what is it?" Doc Josie asked, rushing into the room, Jade right behind her.

"I think I upset her, Doc. I'm so sorry, I didn't mean to."

The doctor froze, her gaze on where Rikki was clutching tightly to Raven's hand. Rikki made another sound of distress, and Josie ordered, "Jade, get Angel. Now."

"I already let her know what's going on, but I'll go make sure she's coming."

When Jade ran from the room, Raven cried, "I really am sorry!"

Doc Josie grinned, shaking her head in excitement. "Raven, I don't know what the hell you did, but keep it going."

"What?"

"She hasn't moved in months. Nothing."

Raven sat in shocked silence for a moment, unsure what to say. When Rikki moaned, her eyebrows furrowing as if she were in pain, Raven rose and ran a hand over her brow. "I was just talking to her."

"What about?" Angel demanded, as she breezed into the room, the entire RARE team on her heels.

"I... I..." Raven was so flustered, she didn't know what to say. Her eyes went to Jaxson imploringly, and then Rikki let out another moan, squeezing her hand so hard Raven gasped.

"Are you okay?" Jaxson demanded, crossing the room and reaching for her hand, as if to pull it away from Rikki's.

"No!" Doc Josie snapped, grabbing his arm. "I haven't seen Rikki do anything like this in a long time. Don't interrupt."

"But she's hurting my mate," Jaxson snarled, his gaze going from Raven to Rikki, uncertainty on his face.

Rikki whimpered, and began thrashing her head back and forth on the pillow. "No!" she mumbled, her breathing becoming labored. "No!"

"Raven, this is very important. What were you talking to her about?" Doc Josie asked.

"Nothing," Raven whispered, tears filling her eyes as she looked down at Rikki. "I just wanted to meet her. I told her I was Jaxson's mate, and that..." Her voice trailed off as her eyes widened in comprehension. "Oh!" Leaning in close, Raven gently stroked Rikki's hair as she told her, "Rikki, I promise you, I'm all right now. I'm here... with Jaxson and the rest of RARE. I'm a part of the White River Wolves pack. I'm safe. No harm will come to me ever again."

Slowly, Rikki's struggling began to subside, her grip on Raven's hand loosening, but not breaking away. Raven kept running a hand over the other woman's hair until she was sure Rikki was calm, and then she slowly straightened and looked at the others in the room. "I told her you saved me from the General. That must have been what triggered her reaction. I didn't realize, or I never would have said anything."

"I, for one, am glad you did," the doctor said, a wide grin on her face. "And, I think you need to sit back down and tell her the rest of your story. It's one she needs to hear."

Raven bit her lip nervously, then asked, "Are you sure? I don't want to upset her anymore."

"Raven, if you can get that kind of reaction out of our girl, you tell her whatever the hell you want," Angel said, her eyes wet with unshed tears. "Please."

Nodding slowly, Raven sat back down in the chair, her eyes going to Jaxson. "Okay, if you are sure."

"Positive," Angel said, crossing the room to give her a quick hug, before leaving, wiping her eyes on the way out.

Jaxson leaned down and kissed her softly. "Thank you."

"For what?"

"For being you."

When Jaxson walked into his apartment three hours later, he stopped in surprise at the sight that greeted him. His heart began to pound as he followed the trail of deep red rose petals from the front door back to the bedroom, remembering what happed the last time they had roses in their room. His cock became instantly hard, and he reached down to rearrange himself in his jeans.

"Raven?" He said her name as he pushed open the bedroom door, inhaling her scent mixed with the roses deeply, a low growl slipping free. He wanted her. He always wanted her. Then, his nose twitched slightly when he noticed a subtle change in his mate's scent, and he frowned in confusion.

"You're home," Raven whispered, turning from where she was staring out the window. She was a vision of beauty, in a long, silky light blue nightgown, her hair in waves down her back, her amber eyes wide as they watched him. A soft smile crossed her lips as she held out a hand to him. "I've been waiting for you."

Jaxson slowly crossed the room to her, taking her hand in his as his gaze raked over her from head to foot. "You are so beautiful, baby." Breathing in her scent again, he paused, "Something's off."

Raven's face lit up in a breath-taking smile, and she placed his hand on her stomach. "No, my love, everything is perfect."

"What?"

"I began to suspect a week or so ago that we were going to be adding to our family," she said, ducking her head shyly. "The doctor confirmed it today. I hope it makes you as happy as it makes me."

Jaxson caught his breath, then dropped to his knees, breathing in deeply. "Raven," he managed to choke out. "My sweet Raven."

Sliding her fingers in his hair, she smiled through the tears he could see gathered in her eyes. "After everything that was done to me, I didn't know if it was possible for me to have children. I am so blessed."

"We are blessed," Jaxson rasped, laying his head against her stomach. His own eyes misted over with tears as he thought about the life forming inside her right now. He had no idea how the hell he had gotten so lucky, but he was going to do everything in his power for the rest of his life to make his woman happy.

"Jaxson," she whispered, kneeling down so they were face to face. "I love you."

"I love you, too, my sweet mate."

"You ready?"

Raven glanced over at Jaxson and grinned with excitement. "Yes!" She was about to shift into her dragon for the first time in over a year and she couldn't wait. She knew it would go a long way toward healing not only what was left of her physical wounds, but also the emotional scars she carried with her everywhere. Even with Jaxson wrapped tightly around her, she still had nightmares almost every night. The General was gone, but Ebony was out there. Even though she'd told Jinx that Raven would be free, a part of Raven was having a hard time believing it.

"Let's go!" Jaxson encouraged, laughing. "Show me your beautiful dragon, mate."

Glancing around to make sure they were alone, Raven grasped the hem of her shirt and slid it up over her head. Her fingers trembled as she removed her shoes and pants. Raven could feel her dragon pushing at her. She wanted out and was tired of waiting.

"You better hurry," Jaxson growled, "or you aren't going to make it to the shifting part right now."

Raven's eyes met his, and she gasped at the way his gaze raked over her now naked body. She still struggled with the scars that were scattered across her skin, but Jaxson said he loved everything about her, and they were a part of her. They showed the battles she'd gone through and survived. Her skin heated, fire flaring in her, when she remembered the way he'd kissed each one of them just the night before while showing her how beautiful she was to him.

His gaze hot, Jaxson growled her name, "Raven, do you think I'm kidding?" Taking a step toward her, he sliced through his shirt with his claws, quickly ripping it from his body. His hands went to his jeans and she let out a small squeak. "Now, Raven! Shift!"

Closing her eyes, Raven let her dragon take over. It took longer than it used to, but a few minutes later she was standing in front of Jaxson, her red and gold scales laced with orange shining in the bright early morning sun. He stared at her in wonder, then slowly closed the distance between them, reaching out to trace a hand over her neck. Raven blew out a small puff of smoke, rubbing her head against his chest.

"You are so amazing, Raven," he breathed, stroking his hand over her head. "Just stunning."

Raven heard the pride in his voice, and her dragon loved it. So did she. She stepped back and spread her wings wide, nearly moaning in pleasure.

"Go, baby. Fly. Let me see what you look like in the air."

Raven took a step away from him, then another, and

then her dragon took over. She was off the ground before she knew it, soaring into the sky. It was exhilarating, flying high above the ground, the wind rushing past her. After spending so long in a cell, caged like an animal, this was what she needed. It would go a long way toward healing her heart and soul.

Raven heard the loud trumpet to another dragon and responded in kind, love flowing through her as Rubi joined her in the air. Soon, Dax was there, too, and it was as if they were dancing with each other. Raven couldn't remember ever being as happy as she was right at that moment, twirling in the air, looping around her brother and sister as they breathed fire into the sky. The General had come close to ruining her, but now, she had so much to live for.

She heard a loud howl and glanced below to see a large wolf running below them. His multi-colored reddish-brown, grey, and black fur stood out against the green grass, and her heart filled even more as she recognized the eyes staring up at her. Swooping down low, she flew over the top of her mate, racing across the wide-open terrain with him, her heart beating wildly in her chest. She was home. She was finally home.

Amber sat on the hard dirt floor, her legs drawn up, arms wrapped loosely around them. Tears left tracks down her filthy cheeks, her body shaking uncontrollably in the cold. Hunger gnawed at her insides, her throat dry and raw. She had been alone for days now with no food or water, and she didn't know how much longer she was going to survive.

When Ebony took her to the General after finding her with Raven, she'd expected a bullet to the head, which was her sister's specialty. Either that, or to be given to the scientists to experiment on. Neither of those things had happened. Instead, she was taken to a place she'd never been to before and left alone after the first few weeks. She knew there was the very real possibility that she would die of starvation, or possibly even freeze to death. She wondered which would be the worst way to die. Now, she was wishing she'd eaten a bullet.

Amber tried to lick her swollen lips with her tongue, but it didn't help. Nothing she did helped.

She heard the laughter before her sister came into view. At first, she thought she was seeing things as an image of Ebony seemed to waver in front of her. Then, she heard, "So, you are still alive. You're stronger than our useless father thought you were."

There was a loud click, and then the door to the cage she was trapped in slowly creaked open and Ebony walked inside. Amber stared at the silver tips of her sister's black boots, but she stayed quiet.

"He's dead, ya know," Ebony drawled, walking over to squat down in front of her. "I'm in charge now, little sister."

Dread filled her at Ebony's revelation. She was at her sister's mercy. She was afraid that was much worse than her father's.

Ebony lips lifted into an evil smirk. "You know what that means, Amber?" Standing, she began to slowly pace around the confines of the cage. "That means, I get to do whatever the hell I want with you. And you know what I've decided?"

Amber lifted her head, her gaze locking with her sister's, staying silent. No, she didn't know what Ebony had decided, but she knew she was about to find out.

"You have such a soft heart for all those fucking animals you try to save, I'm going to show you what it's like to live like one."

Amber stiffened, but otherwise didn't react to her sister's comment. Fear raced through her, but she refused to let it show.

"Get her out of here," Ebony spat, motioning to someone behind her. "I want her taken to the facility in southern Florida."

Amber couldn't hold back the small cry that left her lips when she was yanked to her feet and shoved out of the cell. She fell to her hands and knees, then tried to struggle back to her feet, but was too weak. One of the other men lifted her, throwing her over his shoulder. "What are we telling them?"

"I will call in my orders directly to the guards there. Go!" When he started to leave, Ebony called out, "Oh, and Amber? Good luck. You're gonna need it."

Amber blocked out her sister's laughter, biting her lip hard to keep the screams of terror from breaking free. She had spent years trying to save the people imprisoned and experimented on by her father. Now, she had just become one of them.

Make sure and visit my website for information on all of my books, and to sign up for my Newsletter where you will receive all of the latest information on new releases, sales, and more!

Website: **http://www.dawnsullivanauthor.com/**

I would love to have you join my reader's group, Author Dawn Sullivan's Rebel Readers, so that we can hang out and chat, and where you will also get sneak peeks of cover reveals, read excerpts before anyone else, and more!

https://www.facebook.com/groups/AuthorDawnSulli vansRebelReaders/

Dawn Sullivan

ABOUT THE AUTHOR

Dawn Sullivan has a wonderful, supportive husband, and three beautiful children. She enjoys spending time with them, which normally involves some baseball, shooting hoops, taking walks, watching movies, and reading.

Her passion for reading began at a very young age and only grew over time. Whether she was bringing home a book from the library or sneaking one of her mother's romance novels to read by the light in the hallway when she was supposed to be sleeping, Dawn always had a book. She reads several different genres and subgenres, but Paranormal Romance and Romantic Suspense are her favorites.

Dawn has always made up stories of her own, and finally decided to start sharing them with others. She hopes everyone enjoys reading them as much as she enjoys writing them.

facebook.com/dawnsullivanauthor

twitter.com/dawn_author

instagram.com/dawn_sullivan_author

OTHER BOOKS BY DAWN SULLIVAN

RARE Series

Book 1 Nico's Heart

Book 2 Phoenix's Fate

Book 3 Trace's Temptation

Book 4 Saving Storm

Book 5 Angel's Destiny

White River Wolves Series

Book 1 Josie's Miracle

Book 2 Slade's Desire

Book 3 Janie's Salvation

Book 4 Sable's Fire

Serenity Springs Series

Book 1 Tempting His Heart

Book 2 Healing Her Spirit

Book 3 Saving His Soul

Book 4 A Caldwell Wedding

Book 5 Keeping Her Trust

Chosen By Destiny

Book 1 Blayke

CPSIA information can be obtained
at www.ICGtesting.com
Printed in the USA
LVHW081403080319
609986LV00035B/619/P